EXIT
STRATEGIES

MEG TODD

© 2021, Meg Todd

All rights reserved. No part of this book may be reproduced, for any reason, by any means, without the permission of the publisher.

Cover design by Doowah Design.
Photo of Meg Todd by Anick Violette.

Earlier versions of many of these stories have been previously published: "My Father's Wife," *Prairie Fire*; "Exit Strategy" *TNQ*; "Maybelle," *The Windsor Review*, "Sisters of Something" ("Daiyu") *Grain Magazine*; "Lot," *Prairie Fire*; "Slaughter," *Humber Literary Review*; "Ruthie," *EVENT Magazine*; "The Naked Man," *Riddle Fence*; "Barrhead" ("New Year's Eve"), *Prairie Fire*; "That Skinnyass Boy," *Grain Magazine*.

This book was printed on Ancient Forest Friendly paper.
Printed and bound in Canada by Hignell Book Printing Inc.

We acknowledge the support of the Canada Council for the Arts and the Manitoba Arts Council for our publishing program.

Library and Archives Canada Cataloguing in Publication

Title: Exit strategies / Meg Todd.
Names: Todd, Meg, author.
Description: Short stories.
Identifiers: Canadiana (print) 20210326344 |
Canadiana (ebook) 20210326352 |
ISBN 9781773240947 (softcover) |
ISBN 9781773240954 (EPUB)
Classification: LCC PS8639.O335 E95 2021 |
DDC C813/.6—dc23

Signature Editions
P.O. Box 206, RPO Corydon, Winnipeg, Manitoba, R3M 3S7
www.signature-editions.com

CONTENTS

Slaughter 9

My Father's Wife 24

Warrior 32

That Skinnyass Boy 38

New Year's Eve 48

Green is the Colour of Calm 63

Maybelle 72

War Zone 83

The Naked Man 98

Ruthie 106

Voice Lessons 117

Daiyu 134

Lot 146

Exit Strategy 161

SLAUGHTER

MY FRIEND JUNE SNOW TALKED ABOUT BUTCHERING THE way other girls talked about cleaning their rooms or baking cookies. She described the procedure, the killing and bleeding and gutting. It had to happen, she said, and she told me I should come to the farm and watch. I loved the farm. There, everything was straightforward and unambiguous, completely different from home, where expectations were loose and rules fluid.

My mother was not impressed by my fascination with June's life. It wasn't so much that she was concerned with the specifics of the slaughter, more that she had no time for country life in general. She didn't understand the allure. She was from Houston, where her father had been a geology professor and her mother a historian. They'd travelled and led rich lives— that's how my mother put it and she meant it as a direct contrast to our life. I didn't really understand because I thought we were rich. June's parents never went anywhere. Her brothers shared a room and all of them had chores and ate oatmeal for breakfast. Mr. Snow drove a truck. His forearms were as thick as my thighs, his hands big and full of nicks and scars. Mrs. Snow wore her hair pulled back in a ponytail with an elastic band and most often when I was there she was mucking out the barn or shovelling dirt or pickling beets. She'd rub her hands on her jeans and blow wayward strands of hair off her face. When I reminded my mother that we had more money than other people she rolled her eyes. "There's rich, Maura, and then there's rich. I'm talking about experience."

That spring my father's cousin came to stay with us. I was eleven and I remember that it was warmer than usual, the kind of spring that's not typical on the prairies, where winter often turns suddenly into an abrupt and unforgiving summer. My mother and I were in the living room—as we were most Sunday afternoons—when my father opened the door, his hand under the elbow of a woman I didn't know. He presented her, Nicole Brasseux, with an unabashed smile, as though she were tulips in November or Belgian chocolates: unusual, special. My mother was lying on her back on the sofa, a book in her hand. And me? I might have been reading, or perhaps working on the puzzle, the sprawling jumble of 2000 pieces that took up the entire coffee table. The picture was of Buckingham Palace with flowers and the Royal Guard in the foreground, but I don't think I ever finished it. In the end I suppose my father packed it away; I must have gotten up one morning to find it gone, the table blank and empty.

My mother had kicked off her slippers. Her exposed toenails gleamed red and her mind was entirely inside her book, nowhere near me or anything close to me. I was used to this. It was my mother's way. But what surprised me was her hesitation at the appearance of this guest. She didn't leap up to welcome Nicole, didn't invite her in; it was as though she withdrew, as though she didn't want to acknowledge something. My father stood in the doorway, expectant, but my mother didn't move. Was she startled? Embarrassed? Was she confused? I wanted to be told what was going on in her mind, what it was that was holding her back. But then the moment passed. My mother put down her book and sat up. She smoothed her hair, smiled in a gush, and moved across the room in her bare feet, hands outstretched in welcome. "Nicole! Darling!" I went to stand beside my mother, who put her arm around me and said, "And this is our Maura."

Nicole, who was somewhere between my mother and me in age, and whom my father had introduced as his "lovely, wayward cousin," wrapped me into silk scarves and long curling hair. She smelled of stale cigarette smoke and travel and I sensed immediately that her arrival was significant. But maybe I'm wrong. Maybe I felt nothing more than the normal excitement of a slight shift in otherwise ordinary circumstances.

In our kitchen that first night, I listened while they reminisced and drank wine. I didn't know the stories and before long I was bored, at which point my mother took it upon herself to explain why I shouldn't be. "Nicole's had an extraordinary childhood, Maura." She meant I should pay attention. "Her father was French-Italian. An artistic type. Bohemian. Do you know what that means? No, I suppose you wouldn't, would you? It's a thing of the past." She paused, thinking, but then, almost immediately, rushed on. "And her parents were soulmates, wouldn't you say, Ed? Utter soulmates, that's what they were." My father smiled and nodded, humouring my mother as he always did, winking at me as though he hadn't thought of this before or as though it didn't matter. This is the way my father was, an observer, not an actor. He was the steady weight to ground my mother, who floated through life, unattached, unfazed. If I scraped my knee or cut my finger, she stopped the bleeding but she never demonstrated concern. For her, the joys and aches of life were equally normal and interesting. "Pay attention to how you respond, how things affect you," she told me. My father was a businessman, often away for work, but even then, when he was not around, I felt somehow that his was the quiet presence that kept us safe.

"Can you imagine what that's like? Meeting your soulmate?" My mother put her hand on top of my father's. He looked down, and then he glanced at Nicole, who was holding a glass of wine and who had her eyes on my mother. "They roamed Europe," my mother went on and her whole body held a kind of contained tension I had never witnessed. "Lived all over like gypsies, right, Nicole? Prague, Amsterdam, Lisbon, Barcelona. Just imagine, Maura—she speaks four languages! I'm right, aren't I?" She put her arm around Nicole and then her voice went quiet. "You've experienced so much more than any of us." Nicole held my mother in an embrace and said something light-hearted. Possibly my mother had tears in her eyes. I didn't understand these emotions and I thought we should sit down and eat dinner. It was late, nine or nine-thirty, and I had homework.

"What about you?" Nicole asked me. "What do you like to do?"

"Maura is a farmer," my mother said, shifting out of sentimentality. Her eyebrows twitched and I could see that she was holding back a laugh. I'd gotten up to open the fridge and pull out delicatessen containers of rice salad and glazed carrots and olives. I transferred things to bowls and set them on the table. My father and Nicole moved to help. "She'd rather be with her friend June than here with us." My mother let my father serve her; she paid no attention, uninterested in the particulars of cooking and housework and the day-to-day predictabilities of life. "Big family," my mother said. She was on her third or fourth glass of wine. "God knows the woman has enough to do without Maura underfoot, but nevertheless, that's where she always is. She's going to a killing." She held her glass to her lips and watched for Nicole's reaction.

"They're butchering in a couple of weeks," my father said. "Claire would like to pretend this sort of thing doesn't happen."

My mother snorted and reached to slap my father's hand, but he caught her wrist, laughed, and then the three of them were laughing.

"They're a nice family," I said, and I helped myself to a piece of bread, spread it with butter. "And June's my friend."

But the conversation had shifted to uncles and second cousins and who'd had a new baby, who'd gotten a divorce. My parents had spent time in England before I was born. My father had family there, and Nicole had spent summer vacations with them. "So many memories." My mother shook her head as she said this, and I could see that her mind was far away from me and from our kitchen.

My mother told me she would have been a lawyer if she could do it all again. She was very much in favour of a complete education for girls. "Don't let anyone stop you, Maura. Your generation—you can do anything you want. Anything." She believed that modern families should live in the city, and when my father could, he took her on trips. They went to New York or Boston or London, my mother in her hat turning and waving to me like she was a carefree debutante. They went to Brazil and when they came back my mother complained about inequality and gave Izzy, the neighbour girl who looked after me while they were gone and who came over to help some mornings, a raise. When they came back from France my mother started drinking red wine in the late afternoons. Always my father laughed and went along.

    We lived on forty acres of uncultivated prairie. My father loved the grasses, the gentle inclines, the scrub trees; he loved the long winters, the hot summers, the deer and coyotes that appeared on the edges of the property. After a trip, he'd stand in front of the house and look out over the prairie for ages, just stand and look. He reminded my mother, gently, that the city was forty-five minutes away, that she had a car. My mother read her books; she listened to music; she bought tickets to the symphony, which visited our city once a year; sometimes she started painting or writing poetry. And every afternoon, she walked. There were no sidewalks where we lived, so she walked on the soft shoulder of the gravel road, taking long fluid strides, with her head high, her arms loose and light. She walked like she was in the city, looking into the distance, tilting her head leisurely right and left as though there was something more to see than the same endless fields she resented. Sometimes, from my bedroom window, I watched her make her way down our long drive, and something about the way she moved reminded me of the postcard she'd sent from Paris. It was black and white with yellow washing over it and the picture was of a café with people leaning back in their little chairs, blowing smoke upward so that the whole image was hazy-soft. My mother walked up the road for thirty minutes and then she turned and walked back down.

Nicole was a vegetarian, and after the first few days, my mother suggested we all eat meat less often. It was the early '70s, and we lived in farm country, where vegetarianism was even more unusual than it would have been in the city. Nicole talked about ethics and humanity, and my mother nodded with enthusiasm while Nicole chopped onions and garlic. She made pasta sauces, experimenting with wilted parsley and chopped olives and capers, homemade meals we'd never had before, and my mother ate with uncharacteristic relish, exclaiming about Nicole's magic.

When I came home from school in the afternoons, the two of them would be at the kitchen table or in the sunroom with their heads together, talking about books or Paris or movies, or people and things I'd never heard of. Nicole would offer me herbal tea and ask about school and teachers and friends. I'd lean against her and she'd stroke my back. I told her that cows have the most understanding eyes in the world and that watching lambs play should make anyone happy.

In June's church they talked about the Lamb of God. It refers to Jesus, June told me. She said that Jesus' death meant that mankind's sins are forgiven. When I first went to church with June's family, I asked my mother to explain things. She shrugged and said that Jesus or no Jesus, there would always be evil in the world. My mother didn't believe in church. She'd get up late on Sundays, lounge in the dining room eating croissants and sipping coffee with hot milk. At that time, where we lived, croissants were hard to find. Most people ate Danishes, which I preferred, but my mother searched hard to find a tiny French bakery on a side street, and Saturday afternoons she'd make the special trip to the city. Sunday morning breakfasts are meant to be slow and civilized, my mother said. She put on classical music and did the crossword, occasionally asking my father and me a definition, never really paying attention to our answers.

June's family was Catholic, and at the church they knew everyone and everyone knew them. Sometimes June walked serious steps to the lectern and did the reading. She spoke slowly and carefully and afterward people patted her on the back and congratulated Mrs. Snow on June's composure. I wasn't allowed to have the wafer and the wine the priest offered at communion. June told me to cross my arms over my chest to receive a blessing. She said I wasn't a member of the family of God. I asked my mother what that meant and she looked at me hard and said, "Tell me this, Maura. What is God? Have you asked June that?" Then she opened her book to stop me from asking anything else. "Never you mind about the Snows and their ideas," she said.

I came home from school one afternoon and Nicole and my mother weren't there. I wandered through the house calling and I felt anxious, a rushed and overwhelming sense of panic. I'd grown used to sharing my day, drinking tea, holding court with Nicole while my mother meandered and dreamed and half-listened.

But they were home. They were in the little bit of garden my mother had cultivated in the backyard, on a bed sheet that was spread into a white square on the grass. My mother was on her back with her head in Nicole's lap. Nicole ran her fingers through my mother's dark hair. Something about the way she was speaking, in a light, musical voice, made me stop, made me wish I hadn't found them. The scene was so beautiful, so perfect.

I felt I shouldn't be there, but it was too late. Nicole turned. "Maura!" And then my mother sat up and stretched one arm toward me. "Darling! Is it that late already?" All around them in the sparse beds, faded tulip petals had fallen. There were only a few of the red flowers that still stood strong and vibrant. Spring was ending.

The night before the slaughter, I asked Nicole if she believed in God. The conversation between my mother and me was ongoing and up until that point it had had more to do with the difference between the Snow family and ours than with anything else. June had told me I should be baptized. She said it didn't matter so much which religion, but that baptism washed away original sin. "When you're in the family of God," she said, "even if you do something wrong—I mean, let's say someone does—then it's still okay because God forgives sinners. That's the whole point." I wanted to stop talking about God and ask June about homework. I'm not sure if I felt uncomfortable with what she was saying or if I genuinely needed help with Science or Math. June had stolen a shirt from Eaton's department store on a Friday after school. My father had dropped us off in the city and we were sitting in the food court eating chocolate malts when she pulled a peasant blouse—the kind that were so fashionable then—out of her bag. I looked at the blouse and looked at her and somehow I felt the blouse was mine, as though she'd stolen it from me and was taunting me. I'd been right there in the store with her and I hadn't seen what she was doing. There was a tightness in my stomach and I couldn't speak. It wasn't so much the stealing; it was that things had changed. More than anything I wanted to take the blouse from her and slip it back onto its hanger and into the rack.

 When I asked Nicole about God I really wanted to tell her about June. I wanted Nicole to forgive June, to say it was all right. I could tell Nicole, I thought, but I couldn't tell my mother because my mother would laugh and point out the irony. Nicole wore gold bracelets to symbolize her belief. "They're perfect circles," she said, lifting her arms so the bracelets clinked, "with no beginning and no end and that's what life is. It just continues. With us or without us. We think we own things, Maura. We think life belongs to us, but it doesn't. Life belongs to no one." She poured herself a glass of water and took a sip. When Nicole put the glass down, her lips were wet and with the back of her hand she wiped away a drop that had escaped from the corner of her mouth. "But I suppose. I suppose we have to believe in something, don't we?" Her words were no answer. I didn't tell her about June.

My mother was coming back from the garage where she'd gone to get a bottle of wine. She came in holding the bottle out in front of her, slightly breathless, her cheeks flushed. She was wearing one of Nicole's scarves around her head. I stared. Because in front of me was not my real mother—this was not the woman who lay on her back on the sofa, reading with one arm trailing on the floor, who looked at my father to complain about my friends and my friends' parents, my school and the inferior education I was getting. "Maura knows more about cows and chickens than she does about the Greeks and Romans, Ed." She used to say things like that and my father would ask her what was wrong with that, perhaps it was more practical, and he would pull her up and put his hand on her waist and draw her in. She would lean back and she would let him kiss her, eventually. I thought she was so beautiful, my mother. Her hair was shiny, cut in a bob that moved with her head, not like my friends' mothers who wore either curlers or ponytails. My mother wore lipstick at home even when she was alone.

She put the wine on the counter. "Like the Catholics—wine takes away sins—can we put it that way? Blood of Christ? Isn't that what they say? In the church?" And then she laughed and passed the bottle to Nicole to open. "Are you sure you want to go tomorrow?" she asked me. "You love those animals." One perfect eyebrow raised, as though I'd been joking and she got it.

I nodded. I was sure. She was happier than she should have been, I thought. Giddy. It was unnatural.

"Maura was just asking me about God," Nicole said, pushing the corkscrew into the cork.

"Hmm?" My mother wasn't listening. She twirled her empty glass, eyes on Nicole, waiting.

I had told my mother that June knew what God was, and that she never had to question things because she was baptized and confirmed, and shouldn't I be baptized too? My mother had looked at me with a watery, vague look as though I wasn't there at all. "There's no such thing as right and wrong," she said. "Life is about being. It's about being true to yourself and responsible for the choices you make. And then true to those choices. It goes around something like that. That's truth."

"Stealing?" I wanted to pull her back, to pin her down, make her accountable to what she was saying. "Or lying? Everyone knows that's wrong. Some things are just wrong."

"Maura." My name sounded like the period at the end of a sentence. "You're being pedantic. Real life is not Sunday church."

I wanted to understand what my mother meant and I suppose in a way I did. In my house I wasn't really a child. My mother read me bits of philosophy, or poetry; we performed scenes from Shakespeare together and laughed until we cried. She bought me canvases that I covered with oil paint and pastels and she hung my paintings everywhere with an enthusiasm better suited to the art of great masters. My mother believed in freedom, that's what I was beginning to realize, but it wasn't something I could explain.

On the day of the slaughter we left the house right after breakfast. Nicole sat in the front seat beside my mother and talked about the bleakness of the landscape. She called it beautiful and said it made her ache, and my mother laughed. "Ache is the perfect word." She meant it wasn't beautiful at all. Barbed wire fences lined the highway. Gophers stood up straight on the shoulder or in the fields or right in the middle of the road and Nicole exclaimed that she'd never seen rodents so bold. She turned to look at me and reached between the seats to put her hand on my knee. "You're a very lucky young lady," she said. "It's not every mother who is willing to sacrifice it all so their child can be brought up in such idyllic..." She paused and my mother smiled with one side of her mouth, eyebrow up. "No, no," Nicole said. "It's bucolic, right?" She leaned toward my mother. "That's the word, right? Bucolic." The way she leaned, the way her fingers trailed and then fell off my knee—it makes me sad, even now. I remember that I felt apart from them, as though they both had forgotten me, suddenly.

The Snow farm was a mix of buildings. They had chickens and sheep and cows. They had two dogs that rushed up and barked at visitors but were harmless. June helped milk the cows on weekends and her chores had to be finished before we could do anything together. When her family ate dinner they talked and argued. They dished up straight from the pans that Mrs. Snow put on the table and nobody used a napkin. June's younger brothers fought so hard it scared me, but Mrs. Snow ignored them or told them to watch out for the furniture. If they were really rough she sent them outside.

  What I remember is that there were four lambs to be slaughtered. June and I had named them Billy, Apollo, Zeus and Rocket. I cried when June told me they would be killed, but June said her dad did it in a painless way and that lamb's meat was what was in the stew we ate last week, the one I liked. "Besides," she said, "how do you think it would work if we let all the animals live? There's only so much room, Maura." They killed the males and kept the females. This year there were only two females and June's brothers cheered as though it were a battle of the sexes. I didn't understand what they thought they'd won if the males were the ones to be killed.

I got out of the car and my mother got out too. She hugged me hard and for a second I thought she was angry, but then she took my face into both her hands and kissed my lips. "A person can adapt to anything." She may well have said this. It was the kind of statement she loved to make.

The dogs barked and ran at me. Hedge, the big one, pushed his nose into my crotch and Scout, the little one, jumped around my feet and pawed at my legs. I patted them both, told them to be quiet and calm down. They stank but I didn't mind. My feet thumped inside my rubber boots and when I got close to the barn, June shouted at me to hurry. I heard the thick bleat of sheep and the crunch of gravel under the car tires as my mother did a U-turn and pulled away. The sun was hard in the sky. It was hotter than usual even for late spring and I lifted the bottom of my sweatshirt and wished I'd worn something lighter. The air smelled of sage and dust and hay, the metal of tractors and balers and tools.

I remember all these things very well; they've become a part of me. But my mother disagrees. She says I've mixed up the discussions about God and the Lamb of God with the slaughter. "It was chickens they killed that day," she said. "Horrible. Chickens in general, really." I paused then. The memory is so acute. But my mother shrugged and told me I was wrong, as though it were that simple. As though it made a difference.

I remember being steps from the barn door when the gun sounded. The clap shattered me and for a second I was completely deaf. Overhead, far away, so that it was a tiny elongated dot, an airplane crossed the sky, leaving behind a white line that split the blue in half. They'd killed the first lamb. I heard a loud shout followed by good-natured protest. They were all inside, the whole Snow family as well as Kenny, the teenager from the farm next door who helped out sometimes, and June's grandpa, Mr. Snow Senior. I went in and saw the pulley hanging from the rafters. Thick ropes wound around a block of wood and a hook hung from it. Mr. Snow was bent over the dead lamb. Apollo. The spot on his forehead was red blood and I could see the tip of his tongue in his partially open mouth. Bits of grain stuck to the pink flesh and the bowl from which he'd been eating lay tipped on its side. I wanted to sink into the sawdust and weep—more out of respect than grief, I think—but I didn't. I walked over to June, who told me I'd missed it and added that now they were going to bleed him. We watched as Mr. Snow and Mr. Snow Senior tied Apollo's hind feet and then lifted him up and attached the hook. They let go as Kenny hoisted Apollo's upside-down body to the rafters. When June's brothers had placed a stainless-steel bucket underneath, Mr. Snow sliced the dead lamb's throat with a knife. The blood ran bright and alive.

My mother didn't come to pick me up. Mrs. Snow asked if I wanted to call, if she should drive me home. I said no, she'll come. She'll come. And I sat down at the end of the driveway to wait. The sun grew heavier, turning the green grass greener, the yellow fields gold. My whole body was hot and wet with sweat. Eventually I got up. I started walking down the road toward home and maybe thirty minutes later when the light was softening and the coyotes yipping at what might have been a full, round moon, I saw headlights and knew it was my father.

That's what I remember.

Izzy started coming every afternoon. She cleaned, cooked dinner, and was there when I got home from school. She stayed over when my father travelled, which was fairly often. He must have missed my mother, but he never spoke badly of her. When she first left, he shocked me with his quiet tears in the evenings when we'd sit in the living room together. He sat in his recliner with a book, staring out of the window too long to be looking at anything, and after a while, he'd leave the room. I spent more time with June's family. Nobody in their house mentioned my mother.

Once, Izzy wasn't there. My father was in the living room and he called out, "Claire! Is that you? Claire?" He was in the big chair, staring at his knees, one hand on the armrest, kneading the fabric, his legs wide. He held a glass in his other hand and there was a stain on the front of his shirt. His pants were creased in the wrong places and he was wearing only one sock. I stood in the doorway and hoped he hadn't noticed me. I wanted to walk away. I didn't want to see my father like this. I wanted to go to the kitchen where Izzy always had something ready, knowing I'd be hungry after school.

"She should have told me." His voice was so heavy. "Why didn't she tell me?" My father sat as though he had no strength, as though his body couldn't hold him up any longer. Head low between his collarbones, limbs lifeless, his face grey and slack. "I should never have brought her here," he said, and the remorse was more than I could take.

"Where's Izzy?" I spoke loudly, angrily. "Shouldn't she be here? You're not supposed to be home yet."

"A free spirit I tried to tame. I tried to make her happy. I thought she was happy. Didn't you think she was happy? She was happy." And then his voice rose. "She was goddamn happy until that goddamn girl came! I should have known, should have seen it. You never could trust her, never really, really trust her." I didn't know if he meant Nicole or my mother. "You and me," he said, "left out to dry, Maura. Hanging in the wind."

I offered to cook something. I was crying. Sobbing all the tears that hadn't come before this. Tears for me, for my father, for the slaughtered animals. I don't know what I thought I'd cook, but I know that I didn't want to stand there, didn't want to look at him. And I thought that he was right, that she had been happy, that, for all her complaining, she'd liked the country, liked being so comfortable in a place where she was indulged in her complaints. Because that's what we did. We indulged her. Both of us.

I didn't lose contact with my mother, but I lost my connection to her. She called, occasionally. On my birthday, or for Christmas. I remember holding the phone to my ear and hearing her breathing. I couldn't picture her. Where she was, what she looked like.

At some point, I asked if she remembered how she'd hugged me. "Before you left me at the slaughter? At first I thought you'd forgotten me. But then I knew. I knew you were gone. I don't know how, but I knew."

"I remember," my mother said slowly, "I remember that you cried when we picked you up and you accused me of cruelty. The chickens ran around headless. You said I should have known better than to let you go. It took Nicole and me ages to calm you down. Do you remember how you hit her? You bruised her arm, I think. But she held you tight all the way home. She would have done that. Held you and let you sob into her lap." It wasn't lambs, she said again, and she told me that my father and I had waved at the airport when she and Nicole left. "We were all involved," my mother said. "I'm quite certain it was a terrible time for all of us."

Realities fold into one another, they shift, become divided, or they get lost altogether, and in the end all that's left are tangled impressions. I have seen lambs slaughtered. I have helped butcher chickens. At some point, I have done both these things, and I know that my mother left with Nicole Brasseux. I was eleven years old. I waited at the side of the road, and even now when I smell prairie sage I am reminded of spring and death, of abandonment and my mother.

MY FATHER'S WIFE

MY FATHER STOOD IN THE DOORWAY HOLDING BACK Boris, who barked like he always did, and introduced us to his mail-order bride, who wore blue work pants, runners, and an enormous winter coat. She had cropped black hair and small uneven teeth. She looked at us, pointed to her nose and said, "Ma Ma."

My sister put her finger in her mouth and I turned back to Snakes and Ladders, which my sister was losing. She was six and I was ten.

Our house changed with the new wife's arrival. Piles and stacks grew along the walls—boxes of salt, newspapers, cans of corn, sacks of rice, empty bottles, bags of discarded clothing, flattened cardboard and metal, shoes. The air was different. The new wife was clean but not scrubbed, clothed but not dressed. Her smells were not ones I associated with freshness and beauty, but nor were they the odours of neglect we were used to. It was efficiency, perhaps. Clean without frills. Nothing extraneous. My mother had smelled warm. Lavender hand cream, stale coffee and buttery fry-ups. Burnt toast. On bad days the warmth turned to heat. The musk of soft rot. On bad days my sister and I rolled the dice for her, choosing the ladder over the snake, willing her to climb and win. I smell her sometimes still. In a grocery store queue, an apartment lobby, a friend's backyard. It catches me sideways.

MY FATHER'S WIFE

Every evening the new wife set a bowl of rice on the table. Rice and watery soup with greens she'd foraged. Breakfast was the same. Soup and rice. She and my father didn't share a language or culture, but one complemented the other. She was starting over even as he was. She had a history. These things I only realize with hindsight. I remember asking my father why he'd brought home this woman who spoke no English and pulled weeds from the ditch for our soup pot. He was on his back under the car and I could only see half of him. One leg, one arm, a segment of his face. If I squinted, all I saw was a shape. His face was shiny and dark with grease. "Look around you," he said finally. "You have so much." His voice wavered. "So much."

There were many things I didn't understand or didn't think about. Why our neighbour, Mrs. Klein, was alone, whether she was angry or disappointed. I didn't know about struggles in the world. I didn't know about trauma, that it can worm its way into your core and go dormant or fester quietly until something triggers a reaction. I didn't understand the implications of my mother's death. That her disposition could be genetic. And my knowledge of China was based on a children's book about a boy who could swallow the sea, written by an American, or a Brit. I didn't know about poverty or oppression or the Cultural Revolution. About the interconnectedness of things and how we fight to extricate ourselves. To move forward. To save ourselves.

My sister and I spent hours at Mrs. Klein's. She had a bar in her basement. Her kitchen was carpeted. The clock on the hall table had a glass dome and a gold base. Figurines of dogs and ballerinas stood in glass cabinets. Mrs. Klein wore high-heeled slippers and shiny flowered dressing gowns, gold necklaces, gold rings. When we knocked, she picked up her frantic Chihuahua and held him to her chest. "Okay, Booboo, okay," she whispered. Booboo wore a rhinestone collar. His eyes were black beads.

In the basement my sister sat on a white upholstered barstool while I flounced in front of the mirrored wall. We ate salty snacks from half-empty packages we found in the cupboards under the counter. Stale but delicious. Bottles on glass shelves gleamed benevolent yellow liquid at us and we were careful not to empty any of the packages completely. I rolled my non-existent hips, fluttered invisible eyelashes, flicked back fine dirty-blonde hair, my mouth in a sultry O. I held a pretend cigarette between what I imagined were elegant fingers. All this because of the other neighbour, Nahla, who was fifteen and had a poster of a feather-haired pop star above her bed. My visits to her were about the way she curled her black hair into ringlets, the way she seduced the mirror with her thick lips, hitched her breasts to a swell and twisted to see her profile. Nahla rolled her eyes if I asked questions like who's in the poster, or is Iraq part of Africa?

I copied Nahla's moves in Mrs. Klein's basement, but my sister preferred her Ladybird books. She didn't look in the mirror. She sat at the counter and read and ignored me.

Nahla showed me the Qur'an in her father's study. The book was huge and lay open on a gleaming wood pedestal.

"You're unclean," she said, running her finger down the page. "You can't touch it."

Nahla's father wore a hat that was flat-topped and round, embroidered and beautiful. He smiled with his eyes only and never said anything more than hello to me. Her mother was equally distant. Nodding with vague recognition. She was American, Nahla said. She wore a dishdasha and had the same luxurious skin as Nahla and her father. They talked to Nahla about social welfare in underdeveloped nations, about war and oil, partnerships and economics.

"They're professors," Nahla said. "Thinking and studying, that's what they do." She offered me flatbread and honey and said there were two boys she liked but one she liked more because he had a car.

In the year after my mother's death, periodic cold sores appeared on my lips. My elbows crusted over, growing creased and bulbous like little grey brains. Sometimes they bled. Maybe these things were already happening when she was alive. I came home from Nahla's and washed my hands. Then my face and behind my ears. I stared at myself in the mirror. I was pale and skinny. There was nothing luxurious about me.

My father's new wife brought home a rusted swing set. She hoisted it up and over the fence, where it landed askew, one leg pointing skyward. My sister watched her pound the metal into alignment day after day. Boris, too, stayed close, eyes mournful. Every once in a while he barked and the new wife swung the hammer his way, nervous of his lumbering bulk. Mornings and afternoons she brewed tea with leaves pried loose from a compressed disk. It steeped on the table and smelled like dust.

I ignored the swing set and the tea and went to Mrs. Klein's.

"You visit that A-rab girl," she said, lengthening the syllables, watching for my reaction, expressionless.

I waited for more, wondering what she meant, watching the Chihuahua who sat in her arms, quivering and ready to leap, one paw raised.

"Go on, then. Bar's what you're here for." She hummed kisses onto the dog's head.

I sat on the shag carpet in the basement and ate softened chips. Maybe she was watching me from somewhere. After our mother died, Mrs. Klein folded her arms across her chest and clucked her tongue, then she led my sister and me into her kitchen. She gave us each a bar of chocolate. "Eat," she said.

"Eat." And so we did. She sat across from us and shook her head steadily. The chocolate gave me a stomach ache.

There was a small pond at the end of our road. Muddy in the spring and next-to-dry in the summer. It zoomed with insects. Dragonflies, mosquitoes, bluebottles, horseflies. My sister and I didn't care. We curled into the mildewed sofa someone had dumped eons ago, slapped and scratched and read comic books. We played I Spy or I tickled my sister's back and made her shiver. Boris waded ankle deep and snapped at flies until he tired of that and collapsed in the grass. We imagined fish leaping. Catching them with our bare hands. On that sofa my sister and I were twins. We thought the same thing at the same time. That's what I believed. We would float away on that rotting sofa. It would carry us to our mother. We'd arrive on a good day. My sister was the spitting image of my mother. Same hair, same eyes. Same everything.

On the school bus, minor battles flared every morning and every afternoon. A fight over a seat, over the noise level, over the window being up or down. Boys in the back flicked lighters, singeing paper or wrappers so that Mr. Elliot shouted and threatened. He was afraid of those kids in the back, but once he made a boy named Digger get out and walk. The bus went silent. But the next day the ruckus was as loud as ever.

    My sister sat three seats ahead of mine and mostly I didn't notice her, but this time I did. I heard her. A string of Chinese came out of her. A whole sentence sliding off her tongue like melting ice cream.

    I glanced around. Caught Nahla's eye. Saw the easy way she shifted in her seat. "That kook hauled off my swing set," she said to the kids around her. "Shoulda seen it. Her walking down the lane with that old thing over her head. It was so busted up even the garbage guys wouldn't take it."

I didn't speak to my sister for three days. Ignored her when she asked what was wrong. I went to Nahla's and we watched TV until her dad came in, his face tight. He changed the channel to the News, where a panel was discussing tensions in the Middle East. He sat with his elbows on his knees, chin in his hands, leaning forward to hear words that meant nothing to me.

That Nahla and I didn't talk about the bus or my sister or the swing set was a given. The bus was a no-man's-land. A free zone. Limbo. Maybe you played with your siblings or your neighbours at home and maybe you talked to them on the bus, sometimes. But mostly you didn't. Because you were getting ready for school, where you didn't acknowledge them at all.

We went to Nahla's room and I twisted her hair around hot rollers. "It's not fair," I said. "We were watching first."

She stared at me for a second. "My grandma lives there," she said. "Right where the war's at."

I focussed on the rollers and said I wished I had black hair like hers, that she was lucky.

Boris was old. He'd always been old but now he was older still. Nails clicking on the floor, filmy eyes seeing nothing more than dark and light. Incontinent. My father's new wife shouted and swatted with newspaper, shooing him outside. I let him back in and stood firm with my hand on his solid neck, shouting back at her, words she may or may not have understood. She shuffled away, muttering something and shaking her head.

I helped Boris onto my bed and my father said, "Please. For peace, love."

"—and rock and roll!" I said, and laughed.

He hauled Boris out of my room and told me to grow up.

I don't know whether I could have stopped the fight. Whether my inability to navigate loneliness and grief blinded me and made me helpless or whether it fuelled the kind of angry bitterness that makes you want something bad to happen. I pulled my jacket on over my pjs and put Boris on the leash. Probably I was going to the pond to sit on the sofa. To close my eyes and float away. My goal would have been that simple, that silly. My sister and the new wife and Nahla and her father and my father and Mrs. Klein, who should put better snacks in her bar cupboards, and why didn't my sister stick with me anymore? And why had my mom gone and done that? I walked, and maybe I didn't see Mrs. Klein right away, or maybe I did. The long coat she wore over her crazy dressing gown, Booboo on the leash barking himself into a frenzy so that Boris had no choice.

I look back now and see the two of us on the lane that linked the houses of my relatively small, relatively eclectic world. Our respective pyjamas covered by coats for protection, our leashed dogs a further buffer against the threats of the greater world. The two of us walking in semi-darkness.

A growl, a lashing out, a quick snap. That's all it took.

"He's old," I shouted. "He can't help it!"

She was old, I think now. But at the time I couldn't distinguish forty from sixty or sixty from eighty any more than I could determine the nuances of grief and illness or see the link between the past and the present.

Mrs. Klein put her hands on her knees and wailed, but I stood dumb. I was remembering my mother. On her back, mouth open, white and wet, Boris standing over her, licking her pale face, whining. My father pushed my sister and me out of the room. The anguished "no, no, no, no." His voice as high as a girl's.

My father's new wife went over. To apologize. To make things right. To offer sympathy. But Mrs. Klein wouldn't open the door so she went on to Nahla's house and Nahla got her dad to help.

"She was standing there shouting Chinese like a lunatic," Nahla told me on the bus the next morning. "Waving her arms and saying, 'Dok! Dok!' She looked like shit. Honestly. Determined shit I guess you could call it. My dad came back and said she has courage, your stepmom. That's what he said."

Later that day, in her kitchen, she told me they were leaving for Iraq. That they might be back, might not. She said it like she didn't care. Like it wouldn't change anything. She pried open a pomegranate, a fruit I'd never seen before. The seeds were sour and my fingers turned red.

Months after the fight, Boris died, and my sister and I went to the pond. We didn't stay long. Horseflies and mosquitoes active as ever. The sofa stinking of decay. My sister was inconsolable and sometimes I'm tempted to interpret those endless tears as the beginning of her slow decline. But of course they weren't. Hindsight isn't 20/20. The past is muddied by layers and layers that pile up over the years. What we remember becomes opaque, reinterpreted again and again by what comes after. My sister's illness took hold quietly, imperceptibly. Her tears on the sofa beside the pond were normal. Nothing more than grief. Boris had died. And before that our mother.

I turned eleven and joined the badminton team. My stepmom and my sister came to watch the tournaments, my sister with her books and Ma Ma with her thermos of tea. Sometimes they cheered. But mostly they were lost in their own thoughts and didn't notice whether I hit the birdie or missed.

WARRIOR

MY AMERICAN COUSIN ARRIVED AT OUR HOUSE WITH half-closed eyes and a swagger that drew in impressionable me but failed to impress my mother. My cousin was adopted. Mixed blood, my aunt had told my parents. She'd said it proudly, as though adopting the dark-haired toddler was laudable and unprecedented. My mother wasn't convinced. Intentions, she said, did not guarantee results. Fifteen years later my cousin was a rebel. Exiled from her home and sent north to spend her grade eleven year with us.

"Bitch got rid of my snake," my cousin said of my aunt. We were sitting on the roof of our garage. She smoked and I watched, fascinated by the impossible rings she blew. The scorn and the confidence. "But check this out." She lifted her shirt and leaned forward to reveal the small of her back, which read *haudenosaunee* in semi-cursive. "Warrior. So fuck them." It wasn't the meaning of the word so much as the audacity: A tattoo! And so close to her bum! I settled back against the crumbling asphalt roof tiles and breathed deeply. Tobacco she called white man's poison. Weed, she told me, was medicine. I never knew which she'd light up, but either way, I was impressed. Besides the smoke, my cousin smelled of sweat and heady femininity, dirty and raw. My mother told her to shower if she wanted breakfast. Histrionics were verboten in our house.

And that's what my mother believed it was—the clothes, the drawl, the attitude—nothing more than song and dance.

She spread herself across my room. Ripped T-shirts and jeans, tattered sneakers, mismatched socks, dirty bras, panties, tampon boxes, nothing was sacred. I took it in happily, lustily. She dressed and undressed while she talked to me in her lazy, deep voice. "They try to pin me down. That's what folks are always trying to do. They wanna *own* me." She stood in front of the mirror, then the window, naked from the waist up, brazen and wonderful, her breasts like great balloons.

At school the boys circled her and the girls kept their distance. I was in a separate building, down the hill, in a whole other world. I was happy to jump Double Dutch at recess, happy if I had ham not peanut butter on my sandwich, happy to get praise from my teacher. But word trickled down to the primary school, so I learned that everybody was interested in my cousin. I kept my head down and glowed with pride. She slept in my room, in the bunk below me. I shared the air with her, felt the bed quiver when she turned in her sleep. I knew she liked comic books, I knew she hated the smell of coffee grounds, I knew her periods seized her vice-like. I knew more than anyone. And wasn't *she* what we were studying? All week my teacher had been talking about the Métis, how they were a mix of white and Native. I would bring my cousin to class. Show her to them.

And then, one boy did more than circle. Long black hair and a sneer. Afraid of nothing. Held back two years in a row, he had the voice of a man and was in and out of foster homes. Some days he came to school, some days he didn't. He showed up at our house, leaning against the doorframe, a cigarette burning in his fingers. The way he looked at me—the half smile, the sliding eyes. I was acutely aware of my mother, who kept her mouth in a tight line and made the extra lunch, the extra bed, who, a month into my cousin's stay, cut all the towels in half, set out margarine instead of butter, turned down the thermostats in the bedrooms despite the early winter chill. I didn't say come in. I left him there and bolted, hissed at my cousin that she'd better hurry, or maybe she'd better not.

"Ya'll gotta learn to calm down," she said. She rooted through the clothes on the floor until she found her sweatshirt, and then she was gone.

Three months after she arrived, she said from the bottom bunk into the dark, "Nance? I'm… I'm not doing so good. You know. Like…" She'd gone to bed early. She wasn't feeling well, she said, dizzy and tired. My mind floundered. It went to flu, then it leapt to ringworm (I'd had a terrible case once, mysterious red, itchy welts on my legs, caught from the barn cats that lived up Johnson's way and that I used to love but that my mother abhorred), then cancer. "Is that it?" I whispered. "Are you dying?" In the silence she let bloom, I thought of life without her, I thought of the uselessness of an empty bottom bunk, the bleakness of a tidy room. Eventually I fell asleep, a smaller version of my cousin dancing in my head, a semi-deflated, cloudy version, one that was in danger of being stepped on, popped.

She disappeared and my mother went from angry to anguished to disparaging. Her face red, her lips tighter than ever. I did my homework, kept my room in order and put away the dishes without being told. Even so, I was reprimanded: My shoes were dirty; I hadn't wiped the sink properly; I didn't know how to manoeuvre a broom. And then she wept and frightened me. An enormous mystery, she called my cousin. "The idea that sending her here would help. The *idea!*" There were endless phone calls. To the police, to my aunt, to the school. There were visits to the boy's foster parents who said they had no knowledge and no control, and no they hadn't seen him but that didn't mean he was missing and it didn't mean he was involved. And there were interrogations of me. There was no way I could be sharing a room with her and not know what was going on. I protested. And I said she'd be back, of course she would be, she was my cousin, she lived with us, she was family. Besides, I said, she's coming to my class. She promised. But she didn't come. I stood at the front of the classroom and apologized. "Can you tell us about her?" my teacher asked. "Her background?" I thought and thought and finally I said, "She has a tattoo." I meant to say that she was brave. I cried myself to sleep and I did not disagree with my mother. I should have known where she'd gone. And she was a mystery. Or she was dead.

And then she reappeared. Came in through the front door one evening while we were at dinner. Took a plate and slid into the empty chair. I looked closely. She seemed tired, but not unhealthy. "Ya'll got no rights over me," she said, defiant as ever. That she wasn't dead was good, great in fact, but I thought she might be wrong. Maybe my parents did have some rights over her. Wasn't she in their house, eating their food? And why hadn't she come to talk to my class, like she'd promised? It was mixed up for me, adoration and disappointment, my mother and my cousin.

"Anyways," my cousin went on, "I got resilience. It's in my blood, that's what."

"Until you don't," my mother said. "And we're left picking up the pieces. No thank you." My mother kept going, her voice growing harder. She talked about responsibility, common courtesy, and blatant insolence, but my father put his hand on her arm.

"You better call home," he said to my cousin. "As in now. Right now, immediately."

My mother stacked the dirty dishes with fierce precision.

"So what," my cousin said to me. "I sorted things, so what do they care? It's got nothing to do with them. Your folks, that prick doctor, everybody." She'd taken up her place in front of the mirror, and was turning left and right, running her hands over her smooth brown belly, over her breasts, which, to me, seemed more swollen than ever. She looked at me slyly. "Do you wanna touch them?" Her eyes held a challenge, almost a taunt, and there was a longing deep inside me. I wanted to please her, that's what I wanted. I wanted to do what my mother wouldn't. To please and impress her. To offer her something.

I might have hesitated the tiniest bit, knowing somewhere in the back of my mind that this was a bad idea. But I didn't allow myself time to reconsider. I pulled down my panties and showed my cousin my pubic hair. A single strand that had sprouted rebelliously almost overnight, appalling and exciting me.

My cousin leaned in. And then she laughed. Laughed so that I grew warm. She took hold of the hair between her thumb and forefinger and deftly, suddenly, plucked it out. Making my eyes water.

In the bathroom, I locked the door and wept. Not because of her. But because of me. Stupid, stupid me. I thought I would never come out. That it was impossible, that I would never live down my childish foolishness, that my cousin would never speak to me again, that she despised me, that she felt nothing but overwhelming disdain for me. But of course I did come out, and of course it wasn't as I thought it would be. The lights were off in my room and at first I didn't see her and I was immediately relieved. But then I did, and I was again relieved. She was in bed. Where she belonged. A bunched-up heap of blanket, the top of her black head the only part of her that was visible. She was crying. I stood still and didn't know what to do. By that time, I knew she wasn't sick, but I didn't know what had happened, why she had gone and why she had come back.

I touched the blanket mound, tentatively. "I'm sorry," I whispered. For the sadness, for whatever had happened to her, for failing her somehow. For me.

"Shit happens," she said and her voice was muffled. "Pain is pain, Nance. Get it in your head."

"I know that. Duh."

"Come in here," she said. And when she lifted the covers a sour, metallic smell wafted out with her warmth.

I felt it then. A crack, a small fissure in the shell. A day earlier, an hour even, I would have climbed in, I would have wanted nothing more than to feel her strong, brown arms around me. It would have meant complete and utter happiness. But not now. I didn't want to, I couldn't. That part of me had drawn inward, receded. I climbed onto the top bunk and lay on my back, still and straight. I could hear my heartbeat as though it was outside of me, a sound I'd never noticed before.

THAT SKINNYASS BOY

I'VE SEEN HIM HANGING AROUND. HE STANDS OUTSIDE the store in jeans that are too loose over his skinny bum, smoking and talking to anyone who pulls up. He's trouble my mom says but then he's knocking on our kitchen door and she lets him in. Everything's going to be all right she says and she holds his elbow and asks him if he wants coffee. Tells me to stop slurping my cereal and says isn't it time you started your math pages?

He stays. Moves into the barn with his garbage bag full of stuff. Pillow that's grey where his head goes. I don't know why he doesn't stay in my brother's room because it's empty but I'm glad he's not in there because it's my brother's room. My brother left four months ago. Drove off in his van with his bicycle leaning against the seat. My mom said everyone's gotta leave sometime.

The boy talks and talks about life and the government and the poachers who shine their headlights at night to catch deer and who say they'll shoot our dog if it goes on their property again. He stays in the attic room in the barn and comes out in the afternoon smiling and sleepy-eyed. What the fuck he says and she doesn't care much about the swear words but if I try I get smacked. I'm supposed to be working on using my words correctly because now she's my teacher and I don't go to school anymore because the teacher told me something divided by zero is zero and she phoned the school to complain. Said Miss Perkins is too stupid to teach and that's why I wasn't learning, not because I'm stupid. I used to share a desk with Faye and Miss Perkins said we were joined at the hip.

When you're stupid kids laugh at you. That's what I tell him when he stands in the kitchen with coffee and she's outside. He grins at me his lopsided way and says no kidding. Tells me you gotta learn how to cope and why do I think my brother left eh? I think about that but I don't answer. She never went in my brother's room even though she comes in my room all the time. I have the rabbit and she has to make sure I feed him which of course I do. My brother squeezed my shoulder before he left and I wanted to hug him but I didn't.

She tells him he should get a job. You can't just be a welfare bum she says. Get a life. You get a life he says and then she slams him hard and she isn't a weakling. Not like him. He always wears no shirt in the house and his bones stick out of him like a chicken carcass. Once she chopped into her thumb when she killed a chicken and I was bawling with all the blood dripping but she just sat down and told me to phone Richard who's our neighbour and who always helps because that's what neighbours are for. He came over and said holy shit are you okay and she said obviously not and then collapsed and I had to stay and make sure the dog didn't eat the dead chicken while Richard took her to the hospital. I put the chicken in the freezer feathers and all and the next day she said that was fine and her hand was bandaged.

    So after she slams him he screams that he's calling the fucking authorities and she just looks at him for a second before she goes to the door and puts on her boots. You don't get your shit together you're out she says and then she heads out to feed the chickens. I close my math book and go upstairs and look out the window at the trees that are heavy and green and yellow and move in colour patterns when the wind blows.

I used to hear my brother's music in the night. Where they sing about tying your mother down. Sometimes when she was shovelling out the coops or mopping the floor she'd be humming the tune. Maybe she hadn't heard the words. The music was loud and kind of more like shouting and when my brother came out of his room he didn't say much but then he never did so it surprises me when that skinnyass boy tells me my brother's cool and asks me where he went and what he's doing. We're talking behind the barn. I'm supposed to get the rhubarb so I have my head down and then he's just there standing in front of me with his arms across his chest. His hands are dirty. How come you don't have a shirt on I say and he tells me it's fucking hot in the barn. No air at all. Sucks the fucking life right out of you. I pick the thickest stalks and look at his feet which are really big. A lot bigger than any feet I've ever seen. Too big for his skinny legs. Rhubarb leaves are poison I say and he says any idiot knows that.

Just because she hit him doesn't mean anything. They sit at the table him and her and talk and she goes quiet and tells him he's got rights and that he doesn't have to go back and that he's old enough to start his own life. She leans forward and puts her work hands that are all creased up with dirt that never comes out on his skinny arms and says you're a smart boy. If you want to make a change you can do it. Show them you can do it. Prove them wrong. They're not the example you need. Make something of your life she says. And I say who are you talking about? Even though I know it's his parents because you see them driving around town in a beat-up truck. The mom leans out the window and shouts at people. Sometimes she says nice things that are weird and sometimes she says mean things and then coughs like her lungs are ripping open.

My mom looks over at me and says mind your own business and practise your spelling words. Complete sentences and every word has to be right. At school they only care about the spelling word I say. They're wrong she says. Don't you think spelling is about every word? So I open my book and pick up my pencil.

Yeah he says fucking spelling is what'll get you places. That's why I got in trouble. Never could spell or read right. That's not your fault she says. You just learn differently. He shrugs. Tell her about Louis Riel she says and then she gets up and goes outside to thin out the raspberry bushes. So he starts and I listen to the story and watch the way his mouth moves and the way his chest muscles twitch when he talks. He has little blonde hairs around his nipples which are pink in his white skin. You're white like an albino I say and he looks at me and sort of smiles but not in a good way. You like that? I look at my books. No I say I don't like white things. What you like Blacks then? Or Chinese? I ask him what Louis Riel was and he says don't tell her I told you but those Indians are real bastards. Lazy bastards. They'll cheat and lie if you let them and that's all they do. Yeah well you lie I say and he looks at me like he's mad and he wants to know what I mean. You're just a little kid he says. You don't know nothing. I know you're stealing I say. Because I've seen him go into the matchbox on the stove where she keeps money for stuff like juice and butter. And then he pinches my arm so I squirm but I don't cry out. His hand is warm on my skin. He slams back his chair and stands up. Watch out! he says and then he goes to the garage and stays there until dinner. He doesn't talk while we eat chicken soup with potatoes. She says what's with you? And he grunts.

He's smoking because it helps him cope she says. But it's also why he's lazy. That's what marijuana does to you. Makes you useless. And I say well how come you let him? And she gives me a hard kind of stare and says everyone needs a chance.

He's growing plants behind the barn. Thinks I don't know but I saw him there on his hands and knees and I went later and looked at flimsy plants that look like peppermint.

It's the local cash crop she says. That's how people here make their money. That or welfare. Too lazy to get real jobs. Thing is now the government's flying over and they can see the plants. She's standing with her hands on her hips looking out the window where you can see the vegetable garden. I know it's a lie because planes are way too high to see anything small like that but afterward I run behind the barn with a towel when there's a plane and I throw the towel over those scrawny plants. I don't even know why I do that.

My brother used to walk me to the school bus. He'd whistle and sometimes he talked about birds and mountains. Someday I'm going to South America he said. Where the birds are big and colourful. And after that I'm going to make some real money. I didn't say anything because I liked hearing my brother's voice and I wanted to ask if he'd take me but I didn't. He said he'd be back maybe at Christmas. But I'm not staying he said.

She sits beside me and listens while I read *Harriet the Spy*. She's knitting a sweater for that skinnyass boy maybe because she's tired of his white chest or because he doesn't have a sweater and the nights are sometimes cold. The needles go faster than anything. When I read a word wrong she tells me the right way without stopping or looking up. Then I recite the times tables. And she tests me. Faster than yesterday.

He comes in. He's standing by the stove watching us and I can see that his eyes are red. I stop. She looks up and keeps knitting. What? she says. What happened? And she waits for a second and doesn't say anything but he just shakes his head a little bit and he's looking down with his arms all long and heavy. And then she drops the knitting right on the floor and goes to him. She puts her arms around him and I see that he's crying and shaking. Just fucking lying there in her bed he says. They found her. The cops did. After that fucker next door waited two days before going over. And the bastard's on a fucking bender somewhere.

They sit down and they don't even know I'm still there and she's forgotten that we only got to the four times table. I fold my hands on my lap and watch them and the dog puts his head on my hands so I move my top hand and put it on his head. He's supposed to eat now. Then they don't say anything. She picks up her knitting and fixes whatever stitches fell off when she dropped it and then she gets up and turns on the kettle. I knew this would happen he says. And he puts his head on the table. She wipes the counter with hard big circles and says four times seven. And I say twenty-eight.

The next day when he comes in it's 7:30. She looks up and I do too because he never comes out of the garage before lunchtime. Shit's gotta happen he says. And she shrugs and says yeah it does that's for sure. Coffee? And he says sure that'd be great and smiles with one side of his mouth. She pats his shoulder. You're better off she says. And then he shrugs. I gotta make money he says. Get outta here. Sounds good she says.

Under my bed there's my shoebox of stuff. I don't usually go under the bed but then I do. I pull it out and open it. It's where the picture is of me and my brother. I'm a baby and he's holding me and his hair is all flat. You can't really see my face. The picture's there but my envelope's not. That's where my money is and now it's gone and I know right away that he stole it. But what I'm really thinking about is the other stuff in the shoebox like the picture and the pamphlet about Kotex and the pictures of naked men and women that I took from the doctor's office when we went to get her thumb stitches out. All my stuff.

So I go behind the barn and he's there on his knees his bare back shining up to the sun the crack of his skinny bum coming out of his jeans. He whips around even though I don't make a sound at all. What are you doing here? he asks. And I say I'm picking rhubarb maybe. Are you spying? he says. I already know all about your plants I say. So? he says. So? I say and we look at each other. You're stealing I say. And then he looks at his knees which are covered in dirt and he sits there for a second before standing up. He's so skinny he's like a goat. He leaps across the ferns and high grass between his plants and the rhubarb and he grabs my hands and pins them up behind me. Pushes my face against the barn holding my hands higher and higher so they hurt and I feel like my arms might get pulled out of their sockets but I don't cry even though my face is rubbing against the wood and I think slivers are sticking in me. I read your little notes he says in my ear so I feel his breath all hot and wet. You want me to kiss you he says. You love me he says. Spitting out love like a swear word. And I feel him pressing hard against my back. I could turn you around he says. I could pull your shorts down he says. So you're naked. You want that? Even though I try not to I'm crying now. I can't help it because my face is burning up against the wood and my arms are ripping. I say no I don't want that. That's what you're thinking he says. You think about me in the night when you're in your bed. You watch me. Spy on me don't you? You're a baby he says. A baby. A scaredy cat. You don't know nothing he says. And then he drops my arms and spins me so I'm looking at him. He puts his hands on his crotch and thrusts his skinny hips at me. Sneers so he looks mean. Keep your fucking little mouth shut he says. You can't even read I whisper. Fuck you he says.

He tells her he's almost got a job almost got it lined up. And she turns around from the counter where she's chopping onions so her eyes are watering and she has to squint a little to keep her nose from burning and I can feel the onions from where I'm sitting at the table reading about photosynthesis which I don't understand so mostly I'm looking out the window. She says what job? And he shrugs so I know he's lying. Some farmers here could use you she says. With the haying. And there's harvest and the clean-up. There's always something. In the winter you could go north. Work on the rigs. There's no way I'm going there he says. I know a guy wrecked his back there they work you so hard. Wrecked it for fucking life. Not like you've got much choice she says and then he kicks at the floor and goes out. But before he slams the door he gives me the look. She shakes her head and chops.

    Why? I say. Why doesn't he have a choice? And she looks at me and stops cutting. She rubs her hands on the towel and sits down and starts on the story about luck and about the things you can't help. Like where you're born or who your parents are and the things you can help and how you can change and I'm not listening anymore. Just swinging my legs back and forth wondering who's sharing the desk with Faye now that I'm not there. And then she puts her hand on my knee and it hurts me so I stop moving my legs and look at her. You're lucky she says. Your grandpa worked for this and because of him we have property. We have tenants. We can do whatever we want. We have options and some people don't. I nod my head but really I know I have to do what she tells me so I look at my science book and see the pictures of plants and the arrows that go up to the sun and come back to the leaves. She gets up and goes to the counter and chops hard and fast and talks the whole time about rent payments and responsibilities and doing your best and I get tired of everything and go upstairs to lie on my bed.

Do we need juice? she asks in the morning because I'm the juice drinker so she always asks me. And before I can think anything I say yes and then I look at her and look at the top of the stove at the matchbox that might be empty and I say no. No we don't. Not now she says. But tomorrow we will. Think ahead because I'm going to the store now. Anything else? I'm at the table with my beads and the string and I'm frozen stupid. I don't say anything and then I say he took it. He did it. My hands are knots on my knees. She looks in the matchbox and then she's pulling on her boots. That's it she says. And I'm thinking yeah and it serves him right.

He's back to sleeping till noon. And he slinks around and does half smiles that make me look at my feet. Hisses at me when she's not looking. Kiss kiss kiss he says. Or he pushes against me so it hurts. One time when she was outside he said do you even know what fuck means?

I go to the door where I can see the barn even though I don't actually want to and I'm thinking about my brother who's driving somewhere on the highway with his windows open so his hair's flying all over the place and I'm thinking I shouldn't have told.

She hauls him outside and slams him into the side of the truck. Slams his skinny body onto the ground. I close my eyes but I can hear him shouting get the fuck away from me you crazy bitch! And I hear her say you had your chance and then he's crying and choking and then I'm crying too. He's so skinny.

She leaves him there and walks to the garden and her steps are big and hard. I see him curled up tight and I watch until he gets onto his knees and spits and spits. Then I turn around and go to the table and push all my beads and the string into the little cloth bag and she comes in with Swiss chard in her hand and the stalk parts are flecked with dirt and the green and red leaves cover her fist. I'm kind of bawling and she says that's life. I start up to my room even though I can hear her calling after me. It's time for your reading young lady. I'm waiting for her to go on. To tell me I'm not going anywhere. That I have to sit right down and open my book. But she doesn't say anything and I go to my room even though I sort of want her to make me open my book. I want her to get mad at me. Shout at me. I let the rabbit out and he tears circles over my bed and across the room.

She makes him go. Drags all his stuff out of the barn and makes a pile of it beside the truck. There's not much. His pillow and a sleeping bag. Some clothes like jeans and old runners and underwear and crumpled socks. There's papers and magazines and his wallet which is thin and brown. He kicks the pile so one runner rolls in the dirt and some papers fly up but then they just fall back down. He looks off into the woods and his face is dirty. When my brother left he carried a duffle bag filled with his clothes. He put it in the back of the van beside the camp stove and the sleeping bag. She helped him put the bicycle in and gave him a box of food with canned soup and rice and things like that. Even chocolate. Then she smiled like he was doing a good thing and watched him drive off. I look at all that boy's stupid stuff lying all jumbled up like a bunch of nothingness and I wish I was grown up. I stand there and stand there and feel just alone. My brother doesn't even know. Doesn't even know about the skinnyass boy.

He was stealing from me she says to Richard when he comes for coffee on Sunday. Yeah? he says. The apple doesn't fall far from the tree. Yeah she says and she does a deep breath like she's tired. He's probably better off somewhere else she says. She glances at me and I'm not sure what she means and if it's a look that Richard understands in the way that grownups understand things. He nods his head for a long time. Don't take it so hard he says. It's not your fault. She's still looking at me so I open my book and I look at the words but I don't read anything.

NEW YEAR'S EVE

IT TAKES US MOST OF THE DAY TO DRIVE TO THE SMALL town where my father is working. Most of the day driving straight north into blowing snow, with my mother leaning forward, chest close to the wheel, shoulders drawn up. "It's not easy," she says. I don't know if she means the driving and the weather or if she's talking about my father who is a seismologist and away most of the winter. We're driving north to surprise him because it's New Year's Eve.

My mother blinks at the windshield, peers into the endless tiny flakes, and chews on her lip. She tells Elly and me to focus, to keep our eyes on the road and watch for ice and signs indicating when we'll have to turn off the highway. All around us it's empty. Fields without colour, stones and gulches and shrubs invisible under the snow. Barbed wire swallowed by drifts. A white mound looks like a hay bale but then it moves and I see it's a horse, the legs long and obvious. Thin, bare trees line the highway, grey and straight as rulers, and the road is just as straight. The Volkswagen heater doesn't really work so we're wearing mitts and boots. I stare into the falling snow and imagine an animal on the road, a sudden obstacle in front of us, or a patch of ice gleaming clear.

If we'd stayed home, we'd be at the Schmidts'. Mrs. Schmidt, with her pleated skirts and sweater sets, wide hips and soft arms, would be kissing my father on both cheeks and hugging my mother tight. She'd be arranging food and moving the furniture around, setting up the card table for her daughters Sophie and Paula, and for Elly and me. She'd give us stickers and markers and paper, guide us into songs and games. I love Mrs. Schmidt, love the way she tsks and frets and fusses over us. She wants us to have fun. Sparkling apple juice, shortbread cookies and fruit cake, a whole table full of food. At midnight she'd serve us glasses half full of bubbling wine and my mother would laugh and say, yes, why not! and then we'd dance like we were free. My father never looks at us while we go half-crazy and toast the New Year at the Schmidts'. He and Mr. Schmidt play chess and focus on keeping their kings safe while the rest of us play silly games and laugh and do charades until Sophie or Paula starts to cry and it's time for us to go home.

But this year we're going to my father's work. The whole drive I look outside and think about loneliness. How the landscape is nothing more than nothing. How if you don't live in the city, you're stuck in the middle of nowhere. I try to imagine the feeling of getting up in the morning, looking out the window and seeing only emptiness. There are no houses along the highway. Twice we pull into a gas station and both times there are semis lined up, their drivers in the coffee shops reading newspapers or just staring. We don't eat there. My mother scoffs when she sees the concave pies behind glass. She's packed sandwiches, mandarin oranges and a thermos of tea, but I wish we were eating fries with ketchup. I wish we were drinking Coke. Eating concave pies.

We turn onto a smaller highway that isn't divided. Hardly any cars go by and the trees are dense, the open spaces few. I wonder how much farther.

And then the car slides right and I feel weightless because the back end has come alive and is sliding on ice that doesn't gleam. Ice I can't see. My mother's hands are frantic, flying in one direction and then the other, and Elly leans forward between the seats. But there's no control. We're on skates, a sled, a crazy carpet going downhill sideways. I hold my breath and the car spins, spins all the way around into the other lane while it floats forward and I look for an oncoming car, holding onto my seat and the door, waiting for a shock. Which comes when the rear end hits the snow packed up on the shoulder and we thud to a stop. Elly and I laugh with nervous relief and I feel a weakness in my legs.

My mother puts her head back and closes her eyes. Then she blows out hard, twists her head from side to side, lifts and releases her shoulders. It isn't something to laugh about, she says. She blows out again and nods, her face stern. Then she restarts the Volkswagen and pulls onto the highway. She shifts into second, carefully, regains speed, slowly, and Elly and I don't move.

The town is small and flat, a scattering of buildings, hardly a place at all. The hotel is in the middle of the town, right on the highway that runs through everything and keeps going north. We get out and my mother stands still for a second, her hand on the car door. She stares at the hotel and then says, "This is where he is staying?" She says it like she isn't sure. A neon sign flashes *DANCERS! *DANCERS! The wheels and mud flaps of the trucks lining the parking lot are caked in crusted, blackened snow.

The hotel is square and plain and the entrance on the corner of the building is a single glass door, no awning, no steps, nothing elaborate or even interesting. It isn't snowing anymore and it's already dark. The clouds are gone. I can see stars for miles. My mother plugs in the block heater, tells us to get the bag, her purse, our books. We walk across the parking lot and our boots crunch a solid noise. The air bites.

Inside the hotel, the floor mat is soaked with melted snow and beyond its edge watery footprints drift across the linoleum. A red garland droops above a brittle poinsettia on the counter, behind which a man sits and flips through a magazine.

NEW YEAR'S EVE

He looks up and asks if he can help. He has to speak up to be heard over hard music that comes from the bar and makes my body pulse. He's balding, but the hair he does have covers his ears and is slick.

My sister puts her hand over her nose. "It stinks," she says and I whisper that she should shut up.

But it does stink and I wish we were at home. Over the past months, pimples have begun to sprout steadily under my bangs, and my armpits are wet even when I'm cold. Three months ago, just before my birthday, my underpants were stained brown for two days no matter how much I wiped. I didn't tell my mother, and then this morning, before we got in the car, I went to the bathroom and saw that my underpants were red. I knew what it was and I took three pads out of my bottom drawer. They'd been given to all the girls in my class when the teacher gave us the talk about reproductive systems and the particular significance of menstruation. I changed into clean underpants, balling up the stained pair and pushing them deep into the corner of the drawer. I opened one of the packages and placed the pad. The other two I put in my jacket pocket. The package indicated I needed a belt or safety pins, but I have no belt and no safety pins. The pad shifts when I sit or stand or walk and now, in this horrible lobby, I can feel the thick fullness between my legs. I want my mother to say something or do something that will make me feel like we're supposed to be here and that everything will be all right. I need a bathroom.

The man has put down his magazine. "Half-price drinks for the next twenty minutes or so. And $14.95 for the buffet. Mashed potatoes, roast and whatnot, plus you got your pumpkin pie." Then he looks from Elly and me to my mother. "That's what you want, right? 'Cause you can't bring them two in there." He jerks his head to indicate the bar.

"We are here for mine husband," my mother says. "Mr. Baumgartner. He has the crew here. He is the head. The boss of the crew. Stefan. Stefan Baumgartner." She rolls the *r* in our last name so that her voice has to climb over the *t* and the *n*. *Th* comes out as *z*.

"Bomgardner," I whisper. The way the man looks at her—why doesn't she notice things like that? Why does she have to be so *German*?

"You mean *Schteve*." He indicates the door opposite the bar. "In there, far as I know."

The door is marked with a label that says Dining Room. Inside the light is as bright as a hospital's. Bare tables and chairs, a harsh soap and stale grease smell. My father is sitting alone against the far wall with his head down, holding fork and knife, chewing thoroughly. There's a glass of water beside his plate. We pause for a second in the entrance and then Elly clumps across the room. "Papa!" She takes the chair beside my father and leans into him. Some of the tables have dirty dishes on them. The floor isn't clean. Napkins, a spoon, a plastic bag, a ball cap.

"We are so late," my mother says. "I am sorry for this. I had thought… Well. I thought we would… That we could eat together. Perhaps. To celebrate a little."

I look at her, and then look down because even though she's smiling, her voice is unsteady.

"We drove all the way," she says. "For the surprise."

"And we did a spin on the highway. The whole way round," Elly says. "The *whole* way."

My father takes his last bite, the plate scraped clean. His eyes say nothing. My mother nods and presses her lips together. "All right," she says. "*Ja*. But we are fine."

We are the only people in the dining room.

"I have eaten," my father says, touching a paper napkin to his lips, folding it and laying it beside his plate. "As you can see, I am finished." He places his fork and knife at three o'clock, like we do at home. Runs his hand over his chin. "This is not a place for you," he says. "It's not…" His eyes flit to Elly and me, and I see the shake of his head, which is more serious, more negative, because it's so small. "I am sorry."

NEW YEAR'S EVE

"It is New Year's Eve." My mother says this as though he may have forgotten. "And you are not far. Not too far. And so we thought…I thought. That this would be a nice thing."

When we've ordered and the waitress has brought us our burgers and my mother's grilled cheese, my father watches us eat and no one speaks. I hear every bite, feel every crumb, every bit of the tomato and the lettuce and the meat, and what I taste most is the stale odour of the restaurant. My mother's shoulders have drooped and even her hair looks tired.

Afterward, when we pass through the lobby, we see people drifting in and out of the bar, laughing and talking and shouting. Every time the door opens there's a warm waft of booze and cigarettes and sweat. The light is hazy-coloured smoke, dreaminess and make-believe. Men and women move to the beat with thrusts—cowboy hats and bare legs, hair and lipstick, everything pressed together. It's the easy abandonment of reserve that makes me hurt and wish my father was wearing jeans and an open-necked shirt, that he was in the bar with one arm high in the air and the other around my mother, sloppy and happy like all these people.

We go up a flight of stairs and down a narrow hallway. The room smells of smoke and the window is open.

"This?" my mother asks. She doesn't move from the doorway, doesn't come in. "It is so cold, Stefan. Like outside. And" —she indicates with her arm— "there is nothing."

"Leave it," my father says when I reach to close the window. If I blow out quickly, I can see my breath. I press my boots into the baseboard heater that's blowing warm air under the window. Outside it's the smell of diesel and the sound of truck engines.

"They run all night, those trucks," my father says, watching me.

"Well." My mother shakes her head. *"Ich weiss nicht."* She's holding herself so straight, so tight. I'm wondering what she expected, what she thought the room would be like, the place.

Because how could she not have known? She rubs her hands up and down the outsides of her arms. She's going to cry, I'm sure, and it makes me feel angry. Or afraid. Embarrassed for her.

"Stefan?"

My father nods slowly and then he goes to my mother and together they leave the room.

It feels colder then. Even more stark. I stay by the window. The far bed has been slept in. My father has pulled the covers up, tidied, put his work boots in the corner on newspaper, hung his parka and snow pants over the chair. Elly takes out her book, and I wonder if my father and mother have gone to get a new room. If they're going to straighten things out, move us to a hotel where there are TVs, where the rooms are warm, with soft sofas, where the beds have extra pillows and things that hotels have. A swimming pool. A hot tub.

I go into the bathroom and close the door tight. The toilet seat is cracked and the bowl is brown. The water is brown. I undo my zipper and pull down my pants. The pad is red and also reddish-brown. It smells like fish and metal and a humid sweetness. Blood has seeped onto the edges of my underpants and my jeans, forming dark spots on the denim. The walls around the toilet are stained with yellow-orange splatters and I hover above the seat in a squat, afraid to touch anything. I wipe. The water is shockingly red. I flush. But the water doesn't really drain. It swirls slowly, round and round and then it stops. I flush again and this time the water rises before it stops. The pad in my hand is heavy and horrible. I wrap it in toilet paper, more and more toilet paper, and put it in the pocket of my jacket. I place a new pad on my stained underpants and pull them up tight to hold it in place.

Elly is on her back on one of the two double beds. She's eight years old. She has braids that my mother redoes every morning. When my sister's hair is loose, it floats around her, see-through and feathery, and she looks like an angel. Pure, as though nothing can touch her.

NEW YEAR'S EVE

I walk past the bed and go to stand by the heater. I haven't taken off my boots or my jacket. Outside everything is dark and frozen. I stick my head out the window and breathe. Behind me, my sister doesn't move. She's in another world, oblivious to the room, to our parents, to me. I take the pad out of my pocket, smell the rawness that's come from me, and then I'm halfway out of the window, flinging the thing as far as I can. So that it's gone. The air is cold in my throat.

I slide the window closed tight and pull my hands inside my sleeves. "Where's Papa and Mum anyways?" I ask. "Where did they go?"

My sister looks at me as though she's surprised I'm in the room. "I don't know," she says. The clock between the beds reads 10:45. A little more than an hour until midnight.

I sit on the edge of the bed beside my sister and press my thighs together. "The toilet doesn't flush," I say.

Elly doesn't answer so I say nothing more. I take off my jacket and boots and get into bed in my socks and jeans and turtleneck and sweater. I tell my sister to get under the covers so we can get warm and she does this while she reads, turning onto her side, away from me. I press one hand between my legs to keep the pad from shifting. At home we'd be doing charades and I'd be full of cookies and nuts and cheese and dried apricots and for a little while, with Mrs. Schmidt and my mother laughing, with us playing and joking and eating, and with my father and Mr. Schmidt in the corner, involved in their game, I'd be feeling like we're doing the same thing all families do, or something even better. I asked my mother once why we don't see the Schmidts more often. My mother paused before she said, "It is the same like you. You and Elly play at home, but not at school. You have different friends at school. I am not a friend with someone just because she is German." I didn't understand what my mother meant. One year, instead of going to the Schmidts' house for New Year's, they came to ours. My mother put out bowls of nuts and raisins. She lit the candles on the Christmas tree and read stories aloud. There was no dancing, no laughing, no wine at midnight.

They come back and nothing has changed. I don't know where they've been, what they've done. My father picks up his pyjamas and goes into the bathroom. I hold my breath, waiting for him to say something about the blood in the toilet, for him to come out, disgusted and angry. But he doesn't say anything. In his sagging grey and maroon stripes, the pant legs tucked into his wool socks, he says goodnight to Elly and me, telling Elly to put her book down, asking if we've brushed our teeth. My mother rummages in the bag for her toothbrush and nightgown. She undresses with her back to us. Nobody mentions New Year's. My father re-opens the window and turns out the light. Under the covers I feel for Elly's feet, but she pulls them away.

And then I'm wide awake. The music is louder and I hear shouts. The clock reads 1:12. Someone is banging against the wall. Footsteps and solid things move across the floor next door and above us. Noisy voices, people laughing and swearing, sharp explosions. I lie still. Through the half-dark I can see the curve of my father and mother in the next bed. I can hear their steady breaths. My belly is full and cramped, and my thighs hurt. A woman's voice cuts through the music. "Fuck you! *Fuck!* You think I…" I hear glass breaking, and a man shouting, "Bitch! You come near me…" And then a shriek of laughter. The walls move with flashes of light and shouts and music and the noise of trucks starting and braking and honking, people screaming. A siren blasts. Firecrackers that sound like guns.

I'm sweating inside my clothes and I push back the covers, get out of bed, and go to lean out of the window. In the parking lot a group of people are watching two men fight. Cigarette smoke, exhaust from trucks, and steam from the hotel's vents hang heavy. Someone is throwing up. Someone is calling, "You okay? You okay? Are you Dave? Where's Dave?" A woman on the road has her coat wide open; she twirls round and round, beer bottle raised, shouting, "Jesus! Jesus! Hallelujah!" She's in bare feet, and light dances on the horizon behind her. Someone laughs, shouting over and over, "Happy New Year! Happy New Year!" And as background accompaniment, there's the steady hard breathing and pained grunting of the fighting men.

"Ingrid." My father's voice is muffled. "Ignore it. Get into the bed, please."

I do as I'm told, grateful that my father is awake. I pull the covers over my ears even though I don't want them touching my skin.

Then I'm awake again. It's 3:51 and this time I wake with a shock. My father is pulling on his boots, whispering urgent words to my mother, who's half-sitting, holding the covers against her chest, staring at a man who's leaning against our door, moaning, "Steve… Steve…"

I stop breathing. Try to see, to understand.

My father is across the room, pushing the man out the door. "Come on! Stand up, man!"

"It's in… It's 202. 202…. You gotta…"

Is the man crying? Would a grown man be standing in our room crying?

"He's fucking gonna kill her. Steve, I'm telling you! I swear! He's gonna… *fuck!*"

The door closes.

Beside me my mother scrambles into her coat and boots. She goes across the room and opens the door a crack. "Stefan?" she whispers. I hear murmured tension, then nothing. And I don't think. I'm out of bed. Boots on, I follow my mother into the hallway.

A woman is screaming and crying somewhere down the hall. There's no music anymore. No shouting, no firecrackers and fighting, no people. The hallway stinks sour of beer and vomit.

"*Stefan!*" my mother hisses again and I stand just behind her, watching my father help the lurching man move toward the scream. My mother stumbles forward, tripping on her bootlaces, clutching her coat closed. "*Stefan!*" She holds an arm out to keep me from pressing ahead, to protect me. "*Stefan! Where are you going?*" But my father doesn't turn.

We follow him, my mother and I, to the open door at the end of the hall, and there my mother stops. Her hand goes to her mouth. "*Mein Gott. Mein Gott!*"

I hear the woman screaming inside the room and I hear a man moaning and swearing. But what I feel is my father's disgust.

My mother pushes me back. "*Nein!*"

I stand there, in the hallway, held by my mother's hand and by what I've seen. Smoke and bottles and clothes and blankets flung about. A half-naked woman slumped on the floor. A bare mattress. I saw those things. The screaming and swearing continue. I close my eyes tight against all of it. But my father. My father is in that room. In his boots and pyjamas, his hair sticking up with sleep and his hands, naked and open and useless. Pressed against the wall, shivering, my face wet, I squeeze my hands into fists and don't open my eyes. My father. Maybe he's bleeding. Maybe he's dead. Hurt. A woman and the men, all the people in this horrible, horrible hotel leaning over him, kicking him, my father nothing more than a lump huddled small on the floor.

"Mum."

She puts her arms around me. But I've opened my eyes. And I see my father come out of the room holding the woman, who's skinny and naked, wild hair and glass eyes, long white arms and legs and black boots. I see that she's shaking, that there's blood on her face and in her hair. My father looks straight at me. He hasn't fallen. He isn't dead. He pulls a blanket around the woman, and his face is a knot. "Go!" he says, and he jabs a finger in my direction. "Go! Now!"

NEW YEAR'S EVE

My mother urges me back, herding me, pushing me, and my father tightens the blanket. He leads the woman down the hall and I can hear her whimper. Then my father winds up and kicks his whole body at an empty beer bottle. It makes a weak tinkling noise and I turn away, crying huge gulps of air.

Our room flickers green and the way it moves scares me so that I'm sure something has happened to Elly. But no. She's asleep with her hair pulled loose into a halo. My mother bends down and presses her face against Elly's. She holds it there for a long time. Then she straightens and takes a deep breath. She folds her arms over her chest and comes to stand beside me at the window. Green and purple light dances all along the edge of the town, a kind of space-glow streaking upward and it's completely quiet. We stare. The town looks different. Alive and bright and beautiful and I wonder what the light would be like if we were closer, farther north, if it would be more beautiful, or if we'd just stop noticing.

"It's wasted on them," my mother says, shaking her head. "The whole country."

In bed, I can't stop the shivering.

"Close your eyes," my mother says. She tucks me in tighter, her hands firm. "Just roll over and close your eyes."

Once, when I was four or five and couldn't sleep, I asked my mother how I was supposed to go to sleep, how a person went from waking to sleeping. She sat on the edge of my bed, put her hand on my hip and said, "You close your eyes, Ingrid, and you wait. Just wait. Or you can wait with your eyes open. Either way is fine."

I lie still, listening and waiting, and then, eventually, my father comes in. In the green glow, I see him pause at the window before he climbs into bed. My mother shifts against him and then the room is quiet. I close my eyes and see beer bottles and spinning people, fighting men and blood. I see the woman's face, her hair, my underpants, the streaks of colour, red and green and purple.

The next day the sky is a silver-white kind of grey. My mother and Elly and I have boiled eggs and toast in the dining room. And when we're finished a man named Bill drives us up a side-road into nowhere. We turn down a trail in the snow and then we stop in the middle of a field and get out. It isn't snowing, but the light is flat so I can't see if the ground is smooth or bumpy, can't see where the field ends and the sky begins. We've stopped beside my father's truck, a seismic truck with a big box on the back that Bill tells us is the doghouse.

"He shouldn't be long," Bill says. "Checking the wires." He pauses and looks into the whiteness. "It's a holiday," he says. And he shakes his head and gestures for us to go up the steps into the small room that's filled with instruments. My mother thanks him and then we're alone in the doghouse. I watch Bill's truck get smaller and smaller as he drives away.

My mother explains seismic waves and explosions and oil. She describes how cold it gets and how long my father's days are. "He's the only one who knows what must be done," she says and I can feel how much she wants us to understand. Elly and I sit on the two chairs and my mother stands in front of the tiny window and keeps her eyes on the empty field.

"There," she says finally. "There! You see?"

My father is coming towards us. He's a dark spot in the distance and every once in a while, he gets smaller, then he grows again. He's walking, then stooping, then walking. My mother nudges me and nods, so even though I don't want to, I open the door and climb out. Elly follows. My mother stays in the truck.

My socks are wet from sweating at night and my whole body is heavy with sleep that didn't come. By the time we reach my father, I can't feel my feet, and my fingers are numb. My eyebrows are frozen. My father's stubble is white and his breath is a cloud, like Elly's and mine. His eyes sparkle yellow flecks and his cheeks are purple. He's wearing his parka and ski pants and boots and huge gloves, which he takes off every time he moves the wire. He looks at us and nods, but he doesn't say anything. Neither do we. We walk with him.

It's mid-afternoon by the time we're back at the hotel and ready to go. My father puts the bag in the car. "I'm sorry," he says.

My mother lifts her chin and almost smiles.

Two men walk through the parking lot and look at us as if they've met us before. "Have a good time?" one asks, and I look down.

"We watched our papa working," Elly says. As though they might be interested. As though this is a great thing somehow. The men look at my father and I feel small and ugly and naked, and also angry. I want to say something. I want to stand up tall, to tell them…something. I want to kick them. And I want to hide in the back seat of the car and be far away with my mother and my father and Elly. My father scrapes the Volkswagen windows, the noise jarringly brittle in the cold.

"Happy New Year, eh?" one of the men says, and he kicks a chunk of ice.

Only it isn't ice. It's my frozen pad and I watch it roll a mute tumble across the snow, toilet paper loosening and unravelling so that the pad—my soiled pad—half-opens into a stiff canoe shape, a dark stain on the snow. My mother's lips pinch tight and I'm hot and frozen at the same time.

My father puts the scraper inside the car. "Five-thirty," he says to the men's backs. "Tomorrow morning. Don't be late."

One of the men punches the other on the shoulder, laughs and raises his arm. "Heil Hitler!" he says and then both men laugh. They don't look back at my father, who picks up a beer bottle, another bottle, a cigarette package. He picks up my pad. Makes loops with his hand, again and again, catching the toilet paper until he's holding all of it. With his hands full, he leans in and kisses my mother on the cheek, tells her to drive safely.

Three tries and then the car starts. The seats crack with cold. Elly waves and then sinks low in the back seat and opens her book. My father stands in the parking lot and watches us leave.

   When we're miles down the highway, the northern town long gone, I notice the outline of the sun. It's a ghost-sun. I've seen it like that before of course, and sometimes, when it's really cold, a ring appears around it. A sundog. There's no snow blowing at us. The road is quiet and steady and doesn't look at all like the road we were on yesterday. I don't know where we did the 360, can't even imagine it. It's as though we were in a different place altogether, as though yesterday was a long time ago, in someone else's life. I glance at my mother and she doesn't turn her head, but with her right hand she pats my knee and nods as though I've said something.

GREEN IS THE COLOUR OF CALM

1

"Ty says it's abnormal," Britt tells her aunt. "You know, being gay. He says it's like if someone's born without arms or with extra chromosomes or something."

"You can eat those," Melinda says. "The carrot tops. They're edible."

But what Britt wants from her aunt is a reaction, so she keeps going. "He says if procreation is animals' purpose and we're animals, then what's the point?"

Her aunt looks out the window at the apple tree that's leafless and gnarled and which she'll get to soon. Because, she tells Britt, everything has to be pruned.

"Anyways. Are you? I mean. Not that I care."

"Love is about the person," Melinda says.

"Just wondering. Like, no judgement." The carrot tops are like parsley. The same texture in her mouth.

2

"My aunt's totally pathetic," Britt tells Ty. "She asks *me* if she should cut her hair. If she's too old for the long hair thing.

As if I give a shit. It's grey, by the way. Her hair. And she's like a freak about food and stuff."

"Cool."

They're sitting on the ground behind the school, smoking. The air is getting colder and they use Ty's jacket to keep their asses dry. Ty pushed his hand up her shirt once, told her they could get it on right now, right here, between classes. She's known him since before his voice changed. Since before he got braces.

3

At her aunt's she sits next to the window. Because of the so-called toxins.

"Britt… It's terrible for you. Really."

"Really?" Britt inhales deeply, eyes on Melinda. Her aunt loves having her there, loves watching her pull a Coffee Crisp or a bag of Hot Tamales out of her backpack, lick slowly at the candy, chew loudly. And she loves the smoking. It makes her aunt feel better about herself to be concerned about someone else. Britt knows this. They sit across from each other at the kitchen table every few weeks and Melinda asks about Britt's mom.

"The psoriasis? She's not using that cortisone cream, is she? And the counselling? Is she doing that?"

"She's gonna meditate. Supposedly."

"Sugar is the worst possible thing," Melinda says. "Worse than fat."

"Worse than smokes?"

"Well. Maybe. It's possible. Or they're on par. What about the lemon water? Did you tell her that?"

Britt remembers being seven or eight or nine, pinched or punched by Rory, who's four years older and an asshole. She'd started it, he was getting back at her, but no one saw that part. Her mom's fists faster than her thoughts—boom, end of story. But then Melinda leaned in—How do you feel about that? Britt remembers her mom's eyes narrowing. She told Melinda to piss off with her self-righteous horseshit. To mind her own bloody business. Back then Melinda still lived in the city but after that she could stay the hell away from their house, Britt's mom said. Back then Britt's dad was still in the picture. He worked nights and slept in the basement where it was always dark.

4

"You study for Bio?" Ty asks. His notebook is covered with tags. Variations of WRAT and CASPR. He says he's going to med school. Eventually. Britt tells him doctors have no lives and he says depends what kind of doctor. Because he's going for plastics, he says, and reaches for her tits. Fix these, he says, and she crosses her arms. He tells everyone he'll be driving a Ferrari.

"My mom's saying we're gonna foster. Rory gone and all."

"You wanna look at the notes or what?"

She's told him he should come out to Melinda's with her. But she'll never take him. "My mom's not exactly normal," she says.

"No shit."

5

She tells Melinda about making sandwiches for the homeless. How they stood on the sidewalk Thanksgiving Sunday, her mom all smiles, neck stretched with goodness, and then the bums saying, peanut butter and jelly? Is that it? How her mom snapped. Kicked one of the guys in the shins. Ripped the sandwiches out of their hands. But Melinda homes in on the fosters.

"Does she know what she's getting herself into? The approval alone... I mean..."

"I don't know. Maybe. How should I know?"

"Is it the money?" She puts bowls of kefir with blueberries and spirulina on the table. "Of course it is."

"Like you're so perfect."

"Britt?"

She picks up her spoon. The food is supernaturally turquoise.

6

"She lives by herself. My aunt. No friends, nothing," she tells Ty. "'Safe spaces.'" She draws air quotes with her fingers. "That's what she needs. Supposedly. Total loser." They're smoking a joint, drinking beer. Sometimes she thinks he might be an addict. Or have addictive tendencies. Might become an addict. That's the kind of person he is. It used to be football, but now it's dope and booze. He has this way of checking everybody's empties, in case. More than once he's had to be rolled home. Basically.

He talks about the new girl. "She's into techno punk is what I heard."

Britt pulls her knees in tight and then says, "You see her eyes? It's like she's a frigging cat."

"A pussy," Ty says. "Hers." He elbows her. "That's what I'm thinking about." But she says nothing.

He doesn't think things into corners. That's what she likes. What she envies.

7

"Amensalism."

"I don't know."

"Come on, Britt. Try." Melinda is braiding her hair, smoothing each grey, dead-looking bunch right down to the splitting ends, her head tilted, folding and refolding. "Okay. Anomaly," she says, looking at Britt's textbook, which is open on her lap.

"Anomaly means weird."

"But think about it. Scientists learn when things deviate." Melinda doesn't believe in shampoo. Her hair has been grey since she was twenty-seven. "Parasitism," she says.

"I don't even know why I have to learn this shit!"

"It's a base."

"Yeah, right. A base for what?" She yanks open her bag, rummages for her smokes.

"Britt? Everything okay?"

"What do you care?"

Later, Britt tells her aunt the new girl is from the other side of the world. A refugee.

Melinda spreads newspapers on the table and with a knife starts removing the green hull from walnuts. She explains that repetitive activity is good for the brain. "It opens the receptacles," she says.

8

The fosters are sitting in her house a couple of weeks later, like it's theirs. "Cool jacket," the girl says. Practically coming on to her, that sucky. She's blonde and crass—red lipstick and hoop earrings even though she's barely in grade seven. Her teeth are a piece of work. It'd cost a fortune to have them fixed and it's like she knows it, smiling with her mouth closed. The boy is older. He slinks around the high school like he's hoping no one sees him, but at home he's dropping the F-bomb every second word and then he calls Britt's mom a cunt and she breaks his nose. Blood everywhere.

9

Britt presses her lips tight and bounces her knuckles on the table until Melinda tells her to stop already. So she takes out her smokes.

Melinda opens the window. "I bought a ukulele," she says. "Second hand." And then she gets it and starts plucking and singing a French folk song. Her voice is tinny and weird. Until she stops and says, "Your grandpa played the fiddle, you know? And we used to dance. Like hooligans. Your mom with those feet. The quickest." She puts the ukulele back in the corner and Britt doesn't ask, even though she's never heard about her mom and any dancing. Can't imagine.

10

"What happened with you and her anyways? Like. She's your sister."

Her mom dishes up mashed potatoes in round scoops—one for the girl, three for the boy.

"None for me, thanks," Britt says. She looks at the fosters. The girl picks at her food and he's got elbows on the table, shovelling it in. Fucking idiots. As if holding back a thank you is power.

The pot gets clunked into the sink, and when her mom turns back to the table she says, "Well then. Bon appetit."

The girl asks how the Bio test went.

"You got something in your teeth," Britt says.

11

The new girl draws manga in art class. Pixie faces with huge eyes. She signs her drawings, *Oo*, in a double swirl. At her aunt's house, Britt doodles squares over squares, triangles over triangles. She draws circles.

"Some things." Melinda picks up the kettle. "There's not always an answer, that's all. It's not easy. Nothing is." Melinda is all about routine. United Church Sundays, generic prayer group Thursday nights, deep breathing Mondays. She tells Britt there's anonymity in groups. That it's freeing. Nods when she says this. The tea is home-grown thyme. "Your dad," she says. "You ever hear from him? Anything?"

Britt looks out the window. At the brutal apple tree. The bloodied face, broken arm, the way he couldn't shield his head from her mom, that's what she remembers. "Nope," she says. Not even close to real is what she wants to tell the new girl about her drawings. Not even a little bit close.

12

"Don't tell me how good Melinda is," Britt's mom hisses. She drops the bag of walnuts into the trash.

13

"Smoke?" Ty asks.
"Whatever." Britt nods. "Sure, yeah," she says. "Yeah, right? Like, Jesus."
"What's up with you?"
She blows her smoke away from him, watches it disappear. "Chick puked all over the living room," she says. "She's *twelve*. And the dude took off. Clothes, bags, all his shit. Stole twenty bucks and took his pillow. The duvet. Fucking idiots. Social worker's all over it, like, why wasn't anyone home? Why were they drinking? Like…"
"Shit."

14

"A coffee cup. Hit her right in the head. The social worker. And then she went for the girl. Fucked her up too. Blood, the whole thing. And they're like… She's… What am I supposed to…?"
"Oh, *Britt.*"
"Whatever. Anyways, what are *you* gonna do? *Rescue* me? Change the frigging world?"

And then she can't help it. She picks up the jar of pens. It's right there in front of her. She throws it across the room, bawling now. Because what does fucking Melinda care about fucking anything? Standing there. Just standing there. "You should get your stupid hair cut!" she shouts. "You're useless! You know that? Useless!" The jar and the pens roll across the floor until they stop.

15

She holds her arms tight around herself. "It's freezing."
"She's pretty hot though," Ty says. "That new chick."
"They're charging her," she says. "My mom. For sure they're gonna. The cops. Because they showed up yesterday and were all like…"
"Dude." He loosens the laces of his sneakers. Flicks his lighter, rubs his knuckles up and down his thigh.
"Yeah. Whatever."
"What're you gonna do?" he asks.
"Chick asked me to go to the mall with her. That night. So, she coulda been at the mall. With me. So. Yeah."

16

"Sure," her mom says. "Stay with Melinda. Sure. Go find your dad, while you're at it."
"I don't have to go there."
"Damn right you don't."
But she's fifteen. She has to stay somewhere with someone. That's what the social workers tell her.

17

She opens the window and lights a smoke. But she puts it out. Because. "Thing is," she says. "I mean, green eyes, right?"

"What about them?" Melinda's grinding coriander seeds with pestle and bowl.

"This girl."

"The new girl?" She lifts the lid off the lentils when the steam starts to push.

"Ty's all into her. Like woo hoo."

"How does that make you feel?"

Then Britt does light the cigarette. "Two percent of people have green eyes. Two percent."

Melinda stirs the seeds into the lentils. Pulses balance the body's pH is what she says.

18

"So, they gonna make you go to the court thing or what?" His foot quivers steadily, fingers drumming his jeans.

She shrugs. Then she says, "She's my mom."

He grinds his cigarette butt into the ground. "You see that cartoon shit she's into? Like she's a fucking four-year-old."

It's getting too cold to sit outside, breath and smoke the same kind of heavy white. Melinda's started on the apple tree. Because it's dormant, she said. Which is when you tackle it. You find the structure, she said. Take out the dead wood. The suckers. You can see the pattern of Melinda's bones through her T-shirt, right up to her neck, thin as she is. Britt doesn't tell Ty this. She doesn't say anything about the pruning. You're not obligated to go to that hearing, is what Melinda said. You don't owe her anything. She handed Britt a bunch of dead hydrangeas, green and blue. Green is the colour of calm, she said. Maybe Britt will tell the new girl that. Or that Melinda plays the ukulele. That her spine is like a railroad. Like dots on a map.

MAYBELLE

THIS TALL BLACK LADY WITH THREE KIDS COMES IN AND they stand at the counter, the lady asking Vanessa if she can make an appointment because she's just moved here, she has no dentist and she's got a toothache that's not going away. The kids shuffle foot-to-foot close to the lady, except the girl who's older. She sits on the chair and looks at me where I'm standing by the door to the back room, staring at them, so I look at the floor. Thing is, we don't get many black people coming in. The kids are sort of soft-pudgy and they're black as black.

My job every day is the same as yesterday, Vanessa looking at me like I can't do anything and why do I have to be around? You can do whatever you put your mind to is what Mum told me. I want to tell Vanessa that. And the goals they talk about in group— *attainable* goals. If you don't try, you got nothing, guaranteed. The dentist smiles at me usually and says good job even when I'm just standing there waiting for someone to tell me something they want me to do. That's not right, that kind of good job, I get that. You have to earn stuff is what I mean. But I work hard. And I have a job, so I'm lucky that way. Some of them at group have nothing and when we meet and Julie asks about our week and what was good and what wasn't, the ones that have nothing look shrunk. I tell them things like we got new prizes or about the teenager that cried or about the old man losing his dentures or whatever. Sometimes I make up a story because it's better when they smile. Me and Danny drink cups of the coffee after. He walks the beach, picks up all sorts of things, mostly junk, and he doesn't say much. Neither do I but that's fine because group's over and we don't have to talk if we don't want to. Sometimes Danny works. He's one of those guys that stands at the corner, ready. For construction or sometimes shovelling gravel or moving things. Some days he gets picked up.

The lady's from Winnipeg and Vanessa tells her to fill out the form that asks things like does your jaw click and are you allergic to any medications. They'll squeeze her in she says because you can't walk around with a toothache can you? The lady swings up the boy that's holding her leg and sits him on the counter beside the form. And she starts writing. I wink at the boy but he ducks his head so I'm sorry I did that. And then Vanessa smiles like she's nice but not with her eyes so you can tell anyway, and she hands him a pencil but he doesn't take it. "Aren't you a big boy?" she says and he doesn't say anything and neither does the black lady. Vanessa's like that. She hides her lunches in the fridge, puts them in a paper bag that's taped shut and pushes them right to the back behind the half-full bottles of juice and pop and the basket of ketchup packets because she thinks I'll steal her food. Like all fat people steal food.

Sometimes I walk the beach with Danny. They tell us in group that everybody's got problems. That it's all relative. Julie, who's got brown eyes that she opens wide when she's nodding and saying something she wants us to pay attention to, tells us it's about coping, finding the method that works and sticking with it. Routine helps, she says, isn't that right, May? And I say, sure, yeah. And keep my head down and think about the meds and how if they get those wrong you can't cope but I don't say it because we all know that and if we don't it's because they got the meds wrong. Mum died six-and-a-half years ago. Danny gave me a bookshelf he found and also driftwood that curls into antlers. I hauled the driftwood up into my apartment and

Nelson scratches at it, which is fine by me. The bookshelf I left outside because it'd be hard to get up the stairs and because it's too big for my apartment. It melts in the rain. I don't tell Danny I left it but another time he tells me that nothing's made of real wood anymore, it's all particleboard, that's why nothing lasts. He used to be a fisherman. Sometimes he finds hooks or fishing line or plastic can holders. He puts them in the garbage and says people are assholes. Really he's looking for shiny things, he says, treasure the likes of what'll blow your mind.

"Can you watch them, May?" the hygienist asks. I'm not sure what her name is because she's new and not working every time I'm working but she's nice and tells me things to do. Vanessa thinks I'm more bother than help. Keep out of her way is what Julie says. You can't change other people but you can change yourself and when you can't change yourself you have to change the situation. So I always try to stay in the back where I do filing and organize supplies and stuff. But the three kids are in the waiting area because that's where you have to wait. That's where the chairs and books are. So that's where the kids are.

When me and Mum lived in the apartment I used to sit on the back steps and wait for the black baby that lived there. There was pavement where I could skip or play with a ball which I didn't do but sometimes there were kids who did and I'd watch them while I waited. The baby was adopted, Mum told me. When the mum came out with the baby in the stroller I'd help her lift it down the steps. I told Mum I was going to have a black baby. That black babies were the best kind. She said some things are more possible than others. And then she said it's in God's hands, Maybelle. You never know what He'll bring you, but whatever it is, best to be happy and accept because what can you do? That was before she up and died.

"Would that be all right, then?" the hygienist asks and Vanessa shrugs okay, but she looks at me with her eyebrows up like *what the?*

So I get the Mickey Mouse book and sit with the kids and it's tight because I'm not small. The boys might be twins maybe. I open *The Brave Little Tailor* and when I start to read they move in close. Slowly, slowly, and then they're bunching right up to me so they're almost on top of me, arms over my knees. And so I pick them up, one at a time, shift my legs wide, sit them on my lap. Against my chest. I'm not a fast reader but it's okay because they don't mind. Their heads are a mess of little bumps. And then the girl leans in and I put my arm around her so she's not left out. It feels pretty much really good.

I get to the part about the giant trying to squeeze the stone to get water out and when I'm going to read how the giant couldn't do it even though Mickey could because his stone was cheese, the girl pulls her head back and looks up at me, like she's just noticed me, or she's figuring something out. "You're fat," she says.

I keep reading because we're right in the middle of the story.

"Our daddy hates fat people," she says, and I say, "That giant weren't so great as he thought, right? Because no water comes out, did it?"

"*Wasn't* as great," Vanessa says from behind the counter. Which means she's listening. It's a good enough story.

One boy is sucking his thumb, head heavy against me. Like he might fall asleep.

Vanessa gets up to go to the bathroom. She takes the key, which is attached to a toothbrush and which all the patients use and we use too—we don't have any special bathroom or anything—and she looks at me, and says, "If there's a call, could you? I'll be right back."

I tell her, "Sure, no problem." The kids are sticky hot on me. It's like I'm the babysitter. Or the aunty. The way they're comfortable. Maybe they don't even sit with their own mum like this. So when the phone rings I don't move. The girl looks at me like she's waiting for me to get up to do what Vanessa told me, but I don't. I keep right on reading. Anyhow there's voice mail.

Danny says for me to hold onto Mum. She's there all right, he says. But she's not. My apartment's a bachelor. I have Mum's things, like the coffee maker. And the toaster and dishes and all those things. I do the laundry in the basement, which is where everybody does theirs. I do mine Tuesdays. Only saw one person once and I asked if they wanted me to move? But they said, no, it's okay. They'd do it tomorrow. No hurry. I'm twenty-nine years old. I have limitations, mental and physical. But I never talk about Mum at group. I don't know. When I was a kid she used to read to me on her bed. She read until she fell asleep and sometimes when her eyes were closing she'd say things that made no sense. Talking about spaghetti when the book was about mice, or about juice when the book was about fairies. I'd bump her until she woke up. I don't have a dad. Danny says that's too bad, but I say I can't miss something I never had, so it's okay. Sure, he says, I get that. The best book in the world is *Pippi Longstocking*. Pippi, drawing on the floor because the paper was too small to fit a horse. My cat's supposed to be named after the monkey, Mr. Nilsson, but I got it mixed up and called him Nelson. Now that's just his name.

I finish reading and I don't know what to do because we don't have another book. Just magazines. I sit there for a minute. I don't want to move. But the boys start to wiggle around and the girl kicks the leg of the chair. Vanessa's still in the bathroom. I think about holding on to good things, and I say to the kids, "Do you know Pippi? Because I got Pippi." They look at me with kind of nothing looks on their faces, so I say, "Plus, I got a cat." And just like that I scoop them up, take the boys' hands in mine, and with the girl skipping along saying, "Where're we going? What are you doing?" we leave the dentist's office in a tangled knot and I don't think for one second about the next patient or the dentist or Vanessa or the phone or the black lady and we go down the long stairs and out the back door, and then we're in the alley and I blink into the light.

"It's too sunny," the girl says.

"Is this Pip?" one of the boys asks. And I tell them, "Just wait. Just wait."

My apartment's not so far away. Just right down the path, which is actually a trail made by people who want to go to the water but who don't want to go all the way around to the real path where other people go. But even though it's not far, the little guys get draggy and they whine that their feet are sore and that they're tired so I pick them up—one, two—and they hang onto my neck. The girl holds the bottom of my shirt. For a little while I feel big, really, really big, like I might bust open with good feelings.

It takes longer than I think it should and the boys are heavy. I'm breathing hard from the walking and both the little guys are crying and I don't want them to cry. One of them pees his pants, I'm pretty sure, though he keeps shaking his head when I ask him if he has to go and his sister just shrugs her shoulders, which I guess makes sense because it's not her job to know when her brother has to pee. But still.

And then the girl stops. "I'm telling my mum," she says. "Because you're not allowed." Hands in fists. She looks at me and says, "You're not the boss of us."

I kick at her. Because I have to. Because my hands are full with the boys and we have to keep walking so we can read *Pippi* and she has to come.

I know what Julie says. Breathe. You see the stop sign in your head and you take deep breaths. Pause for a bit, right, everyone? Has everyone been practising? Like we're kids. Only practising and doing are not the same. Which is what Danny says. Julie doesn't have a fucking clue what she's talking about, Danny says. Just keep clicking along, May, just keep going. That's what Danny says. So I kick the girl again, the boys are holding my neck tighter, crying harder, all blubber and snot. "We have to go," I shout at her. "Because!" I say. "Because! We're halfway. And you wanted to. You said!"

But already I want to sit down, already I can't go farther and we're just at the path now, the water right there. The water, which is not exactly clean, but which sparkles anyway. The kids see it and one boy points and says, "Boat!" even though there is no boat. He squirms so I let him go and then the other guy wants down and they both run to the water and for a second I'm almost smiling, thinking it's all right, everything's going to be all right and I'm happy to rest my arms which were getting tight and sore. But then I remember that water and kids don't mix. And so I follow them, in a half-run, the girl behind me, crying, and screaming, "We have to go back! I'm telling Mummy! You're a bad lady!"

But the boys are fine. They're good. Standing at the edge, watching the water, waving their hands around and jumping back when the waves push their feet so I sit in the sand because I'm pretty tired.

Water is always better than anything. Even the girl—she sinks into a squatting sit and dips her fingers, makes swirls. She's not screaming and the boys aren't crying.

"Pippi goes in a boat," I say. "A real boat." But the kids don't look at me. I say it again. "There's sharks," I say. And then I shout, "This is not where we're going! We're supposed to read *Pippi*! Remember? About Pippi? And my cat? Because I have a cat!"

The boys don't turn, but the girl does. Her face is plain and naked-honest so I can see pretty clear what she means without her saying anything out loud. She turns away from me again and puts her hands back in the water where she finds a stone, which she throws. Then she finds another one and throws that too.

Walk away. That's Julie in my ears. When you can't change your reactions that's what you do. Sometimes it's as easy as changing what you're looking at, is what Julie says. And that's what I'm doing. I'm not walking away from any kind of bad thing that might happen, but just getting up and going to where there's a bench a little farther up. It's not a real bench, like the kind the city puts in places for people to sit, this is more something somebody wanted to get rid of so they put it there, like you sometimes see an old chair at a bus stop, that kind of thing. I sit. I can see the water and I can half-see the kids as long as they don't go to the right around the side of the bushes that block my view, which they do but by this time I'm just staring at nothing and not thinking anymore about anything.

Then Danny's there like I guess I knew he would be because this time of day, the water's where he's at. I see him coming with his cart a long way off, slowly getting bigger and I think it's good. But then I remember the kids, that I can't see them anymore and I sit on my hands. Because.

He asks me what I'm doing, why I'm not at work.

For a second I blink into the sun and at him. He's big and dark against the light. I try to smile and say nothing. But then I'm telling him and blubbering, "And now they're gone, Danny, and I—"

"Shut up!" he says and he moves back a little. "For fucksake! What the hell?" He tells me to get up, and we walk. He walks faster than me and he's pissed. He looks over his shoulder and tells me that. Real, real pissed. "You messed up," he says. "You fucking messed everything up real good. Whadya go do? Hey?" He pushes his cart with one hand and the other hand is balled up tight and going back and forth, back and forth, which he does sometimes. When he's sort of in a bad way.

"I was looking after them!" I say. "And they liked me, they held onto me. And they was beautiful, Danny. You know, right? Like treasure. Like that." And what I mean is I don't know. "But it wasn't bad," I say. "It wasn't nothing bad. And they wanted to come. They said."

He shakes his head and walks on. "Hey!" he shouts over and over. "Hey! Hey!" Like a crazy man. And I'm pretty sure if the kids are anywhere nears they're going to be scared of him but I don't say that. I go slower so he's way up ahead of me. I'm not sure if he thinks I'm behind him, if he's helping me, or if he's doing something different, going somewhere.

You get what's given to you, Maybelle. Mum said that. Sometimes you have no choice about things. Some days it's like the world has landed on top of me. I tried to tell Danny that once but he told me I wasn't no different from anyone else and to just keep going because somewhere, somewhere there was something worthwhile.

I asked them if they wanted *Pippi* and they said yes. They gave me *permission*. I was going to read to them when we got to the apartment. That's what I was supposed to do, that was my job. Try to see things through the wider lens, Julie says. Like she does with her eyes, is what I think when she says that. Wide lens. I look up, wide, instead of at the sand. But the sun. Gleaming against the water and every single rock so it blinds me. But then. Corner of my eye, in the bushes there, right there, just a bit behind where they were in the first place, I see movement that I know is them. And my whole weight lifts out of my feet. They're there. They're right there, right in front of me, right where I left them almost. I tiptoe. Because. I'm not sure. Just because you never know. And when I lean in and look into the bushes where they're sitting in a circle, I think they might be mad but they're not. They look at me, all three of them with their dark, dark eyes, which are straight-up happy, but then right away, not. Right away more scared than happy and I'm not sure why and wondering for a second if I should go away again.

"Look at this!" the girl says when I just stand there and say nothing. But then it's like she remembers herself, and she plops down in a heap, her back all round and big, just her eyes looking up at me. "We found it so you can't have it," she says.

"It's Pip!" one boy shouts. He gets up and starts to jump. "We got Pip! We got Pip!"

"We have to go," I say. My voice cracks maybe.

The girl moves. She gets onto her knees and shows me what's under her and right away I know it's a Japanese fishing float. A big one. Brown and almost see-through so that it looks old and special. Sometimes Danny finds those, all sizes.

"You can't have it," the girl says again.

"Okay," I say. "I know that. Okay? I know." And I say I have to take them back to the dentist. That it's over.

They don't mind. They get up and walk with me back to the path. The girl holds the float with both hands, out in front of her, but the boys are full of sprung-up energy now. They run ahead, and the way back isn't too far. Nothing like it was before.

"It's a secret," I say then. Because I'm thinking about the dentist and Vanessa who'll be back from the bathroom. And the lady. My words come out fast and my throat hurts. "Okay? You had to go to the bathroom, okay? And we had to wait and you had to pee—I wanted to help you, that's the thing. Why we had to go outside, okay? You had to. So I had to go with you. That's what babysitters do. And mums. They look after you. Even if it's not sitting still and the book and everything doesn't work the way it's supposed to. Because you're okay, aren't you? Nothing bad happened to you. And you had a nice time and the water was fine and nobody got hurt and we're coming back now, aren't we?" I keep talking, keep blabbering all the way up the stairs, telling them they're good, they were good, *I* was good, and there was no problem, they're fine. Aren't they fine and wasn't I nice, wasn't I about to tell the story about Pippi? Wasn't I going to do that? I take them right up the stairs and at the door, I squeeze their little hands hard and I whisper, "Don't you tell. Don't you go doing that."

Vanessa is storming mad but the lady's still not finished. It's like we weren't gone long. Not very long at all even though it felt like a whole day in a kind of place I've never been to before.

Vanessa snatches the kids quicker than quick and she shakes her head at me, hissing, "What did you do?" But the kids ignore her. They run into the room where their mum is talking to the dentist about things like hockey games or government. They don't turn to look at me or say 'bye or anything, which is fine because I have things I have to do.

Vanessa says she's going to fill out an incident report, that my actions are unacceptable, but I'm not really listening to her. I'm thinking about the Japanese float. The way the girl held it like it was a bubble that might bust, and the way every time Danny finds one he shows me and tells me it's lucky and how not just anyone finds lucky stuff. And then I think that maybe this was just about the best day of my life ever and I go into the back to count boxes of gauze and gloves and face masks because inventory is mainly my responsibility.

WAR ZONE

ALL THE WAR TALK AND FOOTAGE OF MIGRANTS AND refugees and suffering makes it that I don't look at the news anymore. I can't. Not that I did before, but sometimes I did and now I don't. Except that in the hotel dining room the TV is always on, so there's no way around it. I look at the floor tiles, which are red-orange square tiles, the tables, which are ordinary wood, and the chairs, which are wood too, with orange padded seats. In the corner there's a buffet under heat lamps. Mum apologizes for the lack of décor, as though this is her fault somehow. On the TV the newscaster speaks French, but the images are the same old story. Mum watches. She dips her factory-made croissant into her coffee, chews and dips and doesn't take her eyes off the screen. It's disgusting, but she's oblivious to the irony—her mouth stuffed full as she watches people who are basically starving. That's the problem with the world. And this trip. Because after the so-called "road trip," she's taking me on a "shopping spree." In London. Denial of inevitable disaster and grief, that's what we're all doing, pretending life is happiness. What she really wants is time in the rental car with me so she can see how I'm doing. I'm not making that up. She told me flat out she's worried about my goals and motivation. The "direction" of my life. And I know that's why she's taking me to London. Her eyes are kind of glassy and she can barely look at me.

I study touch. When you boil it down that's really what it is. But actually it's complicated. Laying on hands, Reiki, positive thoughts, meditation, tuning in to synergy and universal energies, spirituality, alternative methods of healing, listening to the body in a way that conventional medicine doesn't even claim to do. Ordinary people don't understand. There's a lot to learn and it's not easy. So when she's saying, basically, but not in so many words, that it's airy-fairy, I get kind of pissed off.

"You're smart." She doesn't say this, she *pleads* it. "You could be doing anything. You wanted to do international law… and relations…and that kind of thing. Didn't you? Don't you want to do that anymore? I mean… There's that school in Prague—Janey Broach is going there. Deb told me. She says it's excellent. Remember her? She was on your soccer team, wasn't she? They're dealing with real things in her program. Important things. You know what I mean, right? What you could be doing?" Mum's definition of success is a piece of paper in a black frame. Something for people to look at.

Dad is an architect and a couple of years ago, maybe about five, Mum took up interior design so they could work on projects together. Not that they didn't before, but she's all about making things "official." As though she's better at her job now. Their idea of fun is looking at man-made creations, commenting on how they fit or don't fit into the environment, and how they speak to the period in which they were built. Art and religion and history, how it's all connected to whatever's happening in architecture. They're suckers for new products and innovative techniques, and they describe things they like as "architectural," which is their ultimate compliment. Recently she's gotten into these metal screens. She sells them to high-end retail stores and businesses. It's a "niche" she's carved out. That's how she describes it. Filigreed metal patterns she designs and then gets fabricated in China. Her pieces are used as screens and window coverings, art installations and design projects. Like all art, it's useless, but for each design she makes up a "story" she sells and maybe because of that the stuff interests people. But sometimes it's like she forgets she pulls the stories out of thin air. She named me that way. After a girl in some fast-food line-up when she was a teenager. The girl was British, with thick blonde braids and a clean-cut wholesome "vigour" that Mum wanted for her own kid. Yeah, right. Put it this way: my hair is dark brown. There's so much about me she doesn't like but doesn't say straight out. I wear flip-flops, I stopped waxing my arms, leave my hair unwashed, I don't eat meat, I barter whenever possible, I live in communal housing. The list goes on. She tells her friends I'm in Maastricht to study physiotherapy. That I'm close to the top of my class and that although it's not exactly the same as the North American programs, I'm learning essentially the same kind of thing and will be similarly qualified. All of which is bullshit. But she says this as though it would be the measure of something important. As though I, or anyone, would care. "It's a very difficult program," she says. Which is not exactly true, but also not untrue. My program is completely different from Western stuff and we learn conflicting not "congruent" methods. But. It's therapy and it's physical. So, yeah.

"You've got to be careful," she says now. She wipes her mouth, shakes her head. The TV shows people running on a dark street, possibly there's gunfire. I can't tell if it's Europe or the Middle East or where.

"I know that. Obviously."

"Really, Kate. I mean it."

"Please. Don't start with that." If she had her way, I'd never have gone to Europe for school. Never have gone anywhere. Never made friends with anyone whose parents she hadn't vetted personally.

"You just never know," she says.

"Yeah. Except that's not what you're saying. You're saying, basically, that there's ways to know."

"What?"

"Just saying. Whatever. We're all the same is what I mean. We get born, we die. And in between we struggle. Buddhism 101. Think about it."

She laughs. It's her way when the ice gets thin. Laugh and pretend life is fun. A trifle. That's the thing about her and her generation. They're obtuse and completely lacking in sensitivity.

There are migrants all over the place. Trying to get to Britain or America. Out of somewhere and into somewhere else. The situation is updated on the news every day—images of tents and poverty and angry faces. It sort of freaks me out. The desperation. It feels like it could be contagious. I guess I don't know what to think and I feel bad for them and then I think that thinking that's judging, which I'm against on principle. It's one of the things we talk about in school. Although we're not actually supposed to call it school. It's a "centre for sharing." When you're judging someone you're not really looking at them and when you're not really looking at them, it's impossible to contribute to healing. Your own emotional and psychological states can be impediments, they say. Check your bias. Check your "self." Yeah. If I knew what my "self" was.

Our hotel is in this shitty little town that has nothing but a nuclear plant, basically. Mum likes it because it's far away from the migrant camp. That's what I think. She wants to drive to Dieppe, spend the day together, sightsee.

She doesn't go through Calais, because there are queues everywhere, people trying to find the best way to get where they want to go. But we still have to do a stretch on the highway where we get eyed by random people standing in the ditch with their hands out, and where every car gets checked before it goes into the tunnel turn-off. It's creepy. This feeling like you have something someone else wants because you're in a rented Renault shitbox and they're not. I feel almost claustrophobic until we're out of it, on a winding road that's headed into the dunes.

She was quiet in the traffic, but now she says, "How are you feeling about it?" She keeps her eyes on the road, which is narrow with corners where you can't see what might be coming. "Dillon, I mean. Better? Do you want to talk about it?" She's been holding this in since she met me in Brussels. It's that obvious. She's practically quivering with pent-up tension.

"He's an asshole," I say.

"Oh?"

What does she want to know? How he wants an "open" relationship? How he wants me to be more "tuned-in" to sex, more willing to "try" shit?

"Whatever," I say. "It's over. *C'est la vie*. I don't even care."

"Come on, Kate. You've been together two years. You do care. Of course you do. It's a long time—a huge connection—this big part of your life at an important time that's just a big gap now. Have you talked to him? Talking about things helps you sort it, Kate. Really."

"So you're a therapist now?" I turn away from her, stare at the landscape through the side window. Barren hills roll past, on and on, a village that's gone in two seconds, it's that small. Desolate. Not totally ugly. More that it makes you feel lonely. Yellow and greyish-brown colours, rain spitting every once in a while even though the sky is not actually grey.

"What about we pick up some food?" she asks then, and I shrug and don't look at her. Janey Broach's Instagram posts are female couples, her in the arms of tattooed chicks. She believes in free love. I want to say that out loud. I met Dillon at a concert in Germany. Janey was there too. She was with a guy who had a kid named Chad. Four years old with straggly long hair and no shirt, sitting on anyone's lap and telling them how his mum lived in India and was a guru-goddess and how he was named after a country in Africa. He held my hand and asked me if I'd stay with him because he didn't actually like the music. That's when Dillon saw me. Maybe it was the way the kid's hand was in mine, the way the kid made me feel safe and strong. He told me he liked my "confidence." I flirted and fell in love, easily. Janey went from guy to girl to guy, and Dillon and I sat with Chad on a blanket and eventually fell asleep with him, music and fracas all around us. So, yeah. Janey Broach. International relations, important stuff, my ass. Janey Broach has a tat that covers her entire back and she's gained like fifty pounds. A whole lot of free to love.

We pick up baguettes and cheese. I say no to the charcuterie even though I'm hungry and it's local and looks good. She buys two green apples and a slab of chocolate. "Surely?"

I shrug. Of course I eat chocolate and apples. Obviously. Jesus.

"I thought we were going to Dieppe," I say when she stops in a pull-out along an empty stretch of road. "Or at least something more than this. There's nothing here."

"I want to see the bunkers," she says. "This is where wars were fought. It's not that I want to see any place specifically. But so many soldiers died here for so many causes. All around here. Since the Middle Ages even. It's crazy. I just want to see it—I mean the sense of history. To walk where they walked. Plus, it's beautiful. Eerie and tragic, of course, but also beautiful. It adds to the beauty in a way, that kind of loaded history. Don't you think?"

"Whatever. You doing a pilgrimage to Syria too? Or—I don't know—Sudan? Eritria?"

"They were standing up for our freedom, Kate. Yours. Mine. The least we can do is look. We're here."

So I follow her into the dunes and it's not far before we're at this concrete mass which is the bunker and which is camouflaged to look like a grassy mound from all sides including the top. We have to duck our heads to get in and I pretty much think I'm going to be impressed, feel something, just the way it appears out of the hill. We're not the only ones in the semi-dark, empty, concrete space. Two kids and their parents are speaking German, looking through the gaps in the wall facing the Atlantic. We stand behind them and when they leave we lean in to look. The walls are thick and the ocean is miles away. I feel exactly nothing.

She says, "Wow. That's something." And then we leave.

In the car she starts talking about the window openings or whatever you want to call them, and how it's odd that they face west not east and that the layout was not what she'd pictured.

I tell her there was a sign. Which we didn't read.

"Maybe it was to protect what they had," she says, "a kind of reconnaissance place to regroup and make sure everyone's made it? I don't know. But truly, to think of them in there, right? The wind and the rain—a muddy mess I bet. It'd be cold and miserable, that's what I was picturing. The weather would be awful here in the winter. The way it's so open. And that they had to deal with it all in those conditions. The dying all around."

If she doesn't have the story, she makes it up. And she doesn't even know she's doing it. So lame.

Later—when we're down the coast, when the sun has come out and the road has opened up so that we see, once in a while, gaps of blue—we stop again. We're at some kind of nature park that stretches along the water. Cliffs and a huge drop-off to the beach. Trails fork up into the dunes, which are sandy, with low bushes and tall grass. The paths look like they go on forever. Arrows tell us there's a viewpoint at the top and when we get there we're breathing heavy and we're warm. This time we both go to the sign. We stand in front of it and read.

"Oh," she says. "The Germans built them. Not the Allies."

Like that changes something.

"That's why they look west," she says. "I get it. Eleven inches of concrete. Wow. Think about how long it took to build that. Eleven inches. And they're all along the coast. I didn't know. Those Germans, right? German builders. So where were they getting the material and the manpower? That's a lot of stuff, a lot of labour. The French? God, I wish I knew more. Did you study this in high school?"

I shake my head, shrug. What difference does it make? I was looking at the explanation of the view, not the explanation of the landscape, and now I go to the railing to look across the Atlantic at England, which is a thin white line that shines in the sun. It's far away, but seems kind of close. Below me is the beach, where I guess soldiers would have come ashore. To kill, or be killed. It's weird that people want to see this.

She comes to stand beside me and we both look at tankers or ferries or cruise ships—tiny dots on dark blue water that's stippled with whitecaps, and we're so high we can't hear the waves that slide into the huge spread of sand below. Wind whips our hair and makes our eyes water, and then she says, straight into that wind, "So Dad's been diagnosed."

"What?"

She shakes her head and sort of frowns.

Diagnosed, what does that mean? is what I want to say, but the headshake—does it mean she doesn't want to go there, or that she can't hear me? What is she talking about?

I go to ask again—what is she saying? But then I don't because she's turned away from me. And there's something about it. The way she's turned. Her shoulders.

That's how stupid I am. Because she means cancer. Obviously. The glassy eyes, not looking at me. Her plan for this trip. See the war zone and drop the C bomb. Shopping as consolation prize.

Dad's dying.

I stand there staring at the water and then at her and then at the water, waiting, but she says nothing more, so I'm alone with the view of the Atlantic. Diagnosed. Did she already try to tell me this? Some other time? A phone call about a doctor's visit? Or the clinic? He had a cold or something but actually it was more than a cold? Was she talking about this, telling me he was sick? And is it that I wasn't listening because I was thinking about Dillon and how I'm not in touch with myself, and school and how I don't "touch" with enough feeling? Jesus. It's thick as a winter coat this kind of guilt. My armpits are wet. And then I'm shivering.

There's only so long you can look at the ocean. I walk back to the car and get in, and when she opens my door a couple of minutes later it's like the conversation never happened.

"The sun's coming out," she says. "Should we stay and picnic here? A bit into the hills maybe? Find a place out of the wind?"

"Wow."

"What?"

"*I* dissociate? I guess I know where I get it, right? Total disconnect."

"What do you mean?"

"Yeah, Mum. Sure, whatever. Let's picnic. Good idea. Fucking brilliant." I get out of the car and slam the door.

"See how it's already warmer?" she asks. "We just needed the sun to break through." She hoists the handles of the tote bag with food onto her shoulder and chooses one of the little paths that criss-cross the dunes. I march behind her like everything's fine.

The grass pricks at my ankles and shins, and the air has that after-rain freshness thing going on. It's okay. I feel sort of relieved. To be moving, maybe. I don't want her to say anything, but I want to be with her. I guess, maybe. Talking about the weather is perfect. A picnic, fine. Whatever.

And then as we climb higher up the hill, and she still says nothing except "look at those little sage flowers," and "I'm getting hot, aren't you?" I think maybe I got it wrong. Maybe she said, "down-the-coast." "So Dad's been down-the-coast." "Down-this-coast." The wind was loud, distorting things. Just because "diagnose" is on my mind all the time doesn't mean she said it. Last week I interpreted anxiety as a heart attack, the week before, back spasms as MS. My prof told me to pay attention to the whole picture. Not just body language and not just words.

We find a spot that's three quarters of the way up the hill, a sort of alcove. Flat sand with a bank we can lean against. It's nice enough. Warm and quiet and sheltered from the wind. She tears the bread and breaks off hunks of cheese. Somewhere ahead of us is the Atlantic. And England and North America. Behind our backs there's France and Belgium and all of Europe. But what we're looking at is the sandy dune stretching into the sky, which is now completely blue. I concentrate on the moment—the bread, which is typical French, and the cheese, which is pungent and also French. Each bite I chew steadily for a long time, and I focus on visualizing a happy world. The power of the mind. That's what they say in class. They told me to try meditation—let the thoughts come and watch them go, feel it, let it move through you. Healing and the restorative process are, at least in part, dependent on positive mental energy. Happiness is a choice. Health is a state of mind. I know all that, but knowing doesn't actually translate into feeling. Still, it's nice, and I relax.

She finishes the last bit of bread, settles back, turning her face toward the sun, and then she says, "It's his prostate. So, we're not really all that worried. At a certain age, with men, that's just what they get."

It's a second before I can speak. "Oh," I say. Down the coast. Diagnosed. Diagnosed. I knew it.

"You know. It's common. They know how to deal with it."

I push my hands deep and knead the sand, picking up bits of wood, little stones, sifting them through my fingers, letting go first of the sand, then the stones, then the sticks. Breathe. They don't come right out and say it in school, but you can tell. Cancer. It's an obituary. Kiss of death. The end. Cancer's when Western medicine has a place even though Western medicine doesn't know how to deal with it either. That's cancer. Something so internally toxic they have to poison you to try to get rid of it. And there's no guarantee. A crapshoot. Kill everything and hope you live.

I think of the bog people then, suddenly. I saw them with Dad. Last winter break he took me to Ireland to see his grandpa, my great-gramps, who's super old and hard to understand. He didn't really look at me, just at Dad, but that was fine. I drifted through Dublin and thought everyone looked stunted by the weather, which was a thing the whole time we were there and, based on everything from the people to the landscape to the buildings, it looked like it was always a thing. A sky so heavy you didn't even think about reaching. Great-gramps told us to go to the museum of history. He went on and on about it, called it the greatest thing Dublin had, a monument to all the wonderful truths of Ireland. I stood beside Dad and looked at the Celtic gold and weapons and it actually was pretty impressive. Who knew there was so much stuff on that island so long ago? Apparently they threw everything in the bog every time they were invaded, which happened a lot, and that's why there's so much of it, totally preserved. Something like that. And the bog people. How to blow your mind—hair and skin and everything. I couldn't stop looking at them. They're like thousands of years old, before Christ kind of thing, but there they are. The Irish are fighters, Dad said. Hard to take out. He laughed. Great-gramps is 101. His four sons are dead, though. I don't know what they died of. They'd moved to the States or Canada. One lived in Australia. And now Dad will be next. The first of the grandsons.

Beside me Mum digs in her bag and I assume it's for the chocolate or a tissue. But no. What she pulls out is a pack of smokes.

For a second I think it's a joke. That she wants to shock me. Ha. So wrong.

She doesn't look at me until after she's lit one and inhaled. She blows the smoke upward, flicks the ash and says, "Stop looking at me that way." She used to smoke, she says. Before she had me. "I liked it. But I quit. Obviously." She pauses to take a couple of drags and it's the weirdest thing, watching her do this. Like she's someone I don't even know.

"He never did anything bad," she says. "Dad. He's health conscious, morally upright. Ethically…trying to do the right thing. It's…at a certain point…all that denying. Denying yourself things. And the occasional cigarette…so what. Big deal. It's a cigarette. It's not like I'm going to turn into a smoker."

She looks at me hard then, and I see the strict little lines around her mouth and eyes. Her hair is duller than it used to be. She looks old. Leathery. A living bog person.

"So." She stubs out the cigarette against a stone. "Should we walk on for a bit? Or are you ready to go?"

I cross my arms over my chest. My eyes are burning. It's like I'm twelve. Back when I felt like I was an adult, but I wasn't. That totally mixed-up time because you don't know what to feel and nobody's helping you because you don't want them to. But you also do. You want help.

"Kate. Do you want to stay longer?"

"I don't care."

"I don't care either. But I wouldn't mind having some time to get ourselves sorted and packed and all before dinner and before the trek tomorrow. We're going to have to get going early to make it worth our while. What with the delays." She looks at me, squints a bit and then says, "Kate?"

I shake my head, then nod, but I can't speak.

She puts the stupid butt in her pocket and brushes crumbs or ash off her shirt and lap. "Okay," she says. "You're upset. I get that. And I'm sorry. Look. I *am* sorry. I guess it all comes out sounding heavy. But Dad and I aren't that worried. Really. And the doctor says the prognosis is excellent. That's what he said, *excellent*. Honestly. It's just one of those things. Reality check, right? It's like what you say: You live, you die. All of us. It's a reminder. That's a good thing. Think of it that way. It reminds us we're not invincible. And you've got to live, that's the thing. No regrets. Come on, Kate. It's going to be okay. Really."

She turns her head to look at me and smiles, thinking I'm going to say something. I've put my hands back in the sand, which is warm on top but cool underneath. She's waiting for me to shrug and smile and say, "Okay, I get it, Mum, I'm fine now," so we can get going. Talk about it, she says. Talk about it. She's full of shit. But also, maybe not. Maybe he is going to be fine and I should smile. I should say, Okay, let's get going, life is great. But I don't. Because she's smiling, and because the cigarette in her hand was like a raised middle finger.

I go to get up.

"Okay? You ready?"

And as I stand I see where I've been sitting. That the so-called sticks I was holding aren't sticks. They're bones. Right beside me there's a tiny skull with a pointed jaw. Another one, another. And then I see little ribcages, half buried, scattered all around us. I'm freaking out for one millisecond, but then I'm almost laughing. It's like—so appropriate. Little dead animals. Rabbits, I guess. A rabbit graveyard. A war zone. Perfect.

"What's so funny? What are you laughing at?"

I say nothing. And I don't know why I do it, but I pick up one of the bones and hold onto it, rubbing the smoothness as we walk down the hill to the car.

We get back to the hotel and we're tired and wanting time to ourselves. Sick of each other. But the man at the front desk stops us, saying, "Good afternoon," in his accented English. He puts a hand out to keep us from going up the stairs and he hesitates. He's trying to come up with the right words. "There has been…we have…there is…an in-cee-dent."

Migrants is what I think right away. Something's happened. A fight. A death. And then I think of the dead rabbits, the skeletons. But beside me Mum clutches her chest.

"I beg your pardon?" she says. And then she whispers, "What? What incident?" She looks around, crazy like. "Where's my phone?" She's looking at me, rooting in her bag, looking back at me. "Kate! Where's my phone!"

She's afraid.

"Some…some theft have happened," the man says. "So please. Please. It is important you are keeping your handbag and cash with you please. We have security…*mais*…"

She looks at him for a second and then she exhales, and I see the decompression, the complete release.

The man nods, looks confused and nervous. "Madame?" he asks.

"No, no, no," she says. "Sorry. *Je m'excuse. Pardon.*" Her voice cracks. The angst coming through. So that right then I'm sorry for her in a way that makes me feel weak. And also kind of better somehow. Because I get it. And I remember being a little kid. Gripping the climbing bars with the backs of my knees, arms swinging, the hemline of my jungle-print dress brushing my ears, screaming for all I was worth. Faking bravado. Hanging on. Like her. All of us. The migrants. Pushing on even if we're not sure where we're going. If you don't have determination you have nothing, kind of thing.

At dinner the server gives us more details. A few rooms were ransacked, the cash drawer damaged. He shakes his head. "We don't know," he says.

Mum's staring into space, not looking at the menu. "It's desperation," she says. "Or maybe just the temptation. The fact that you *can* do it, so why not. Some people have no self-control that way. A kind of power, I think. Or maybe the guy was supporting a big family? Or he was snooping more than wanting to steal, and the theft was secondary? Accidental even. Poor guy. I mean. Just imagine."

"How do you know it was a guy?" I say.

"Or woman. Sure. Yeah. A woman."

I put my hand on the table. She takes it into hers and we sit there, looking at each other. Mum and me. I want to tell her I'm failing school. That they told me I'm repressed. That Dillon said the same. But I don't. You don't sit down and cry when the soldier in front of you drops, that's the thing. Tomorrow we'll cross the channel. I'll tell her about the bones. Let her make a story—the way the ribcages are shipwrecks. The way the bones have become part of the landscape. The way we're all part of the landscape. The way the world shifts. The fabric of it all. I'll let her talk and then I'll tell her maybe it's not like that at all. Maybe it's remnants of a picnic. Somebody's garbage. And she'll smile and ask if they had a good time, if it was a special occasion, if they'll remember it forever.

THE NAKED MAN

IT WAS SNOWING, BUT SHARONA STAYED ON THE BENCH. She spread the sports section of the newspaper across her lap and unpacked her ham and cheese. The naked man in front of her held his arms extended. His head was tilted right, his mouth slightly open. She ate her sandwich, watching him, and when she was finished she folded the plastic wrap into a tidy square, slid it into the pocket of her duffel coat, and imagined the man's words floating with the snowflakes. "Sharona, Sharona." Silent kisses landing on her hair and nose and hands. Elbows to fingertips his skin was raw pink. Cold fibreglass smoothness. His bare feet didn't feel the snow.

Sharona's days started with coffee and toast. Jam if she'd remembered to buy it. Hot water if she was out of coffee. Sometimes she read romance novels, which she didn't always finish. The College granted library privileges to its employees, and once she took out a classical studies overview, but the sheer volume of information made her droop. Weekdays she took the bus from her apartment and walked the final stretch through residential streets and across campus to the HR department of Yardley Women's College. The College itself was a series of ivy-covered brick buildings on lush grounds, but the Human Resources Building was a worn bunker-like structure in the rear of the property. Her cubicle had no window.

THE NAKED MAN

Her co-workers were mostly youngish women like her and any conversation heading into lunch tended towards which fast food outlet they'd grace and who'd met a new guy and how things were going with the old guy. On the whole, Sharona didn't mind. Janet said Sharona was too passive, that she ought to show her stuff, get out there. "Your looks aren't going to last, sweetheart. Use it or lose it." Mostly, Sharona went along with Janet. But then the man arrived.

He was just there one Monday morning in late December when things were quiet for Christmas, students gone, some of the staff and faculty on vacation. Sharona walked the path across campus and saw him. She stopped and stared. And then she sat down on the bench nearby and stared more. That was the day she stopped going with Janet and the girls for lunch. She bought a sandwich at the cafeteria and ate it on the bench. Beside Raymond, because that was how she thought of the naked man. Naked except for his white Hanes underwear.

Sharona snapped the sports page flat and read aloud about the Seattle Seahawks and their 43-8 Superbowl victory. She didn't know the rules of football, she told Raymond, although of course he didn't answer. His eyes were half-closed. Mid-blink. Her phone rang. She didn't recognize the number, and let it ring. Unrecognized numbers were always the same for Sharona—people looking for rodent removal. Her number was one digit away from Westside Pest Control. It was an ongoing problem.

Later, she listened to the message. It was an Indian accent, a man with squirrels. His voice verged on desperation. *Please call me back immediately*. There was a sense of conviction that she admired: he would have those squirrels removed.

"The thing about you," Janet said, "is you're too untrusting. I mean, look at Veronica. She met a guy online and they dated and everything was fine. Honestly, what's the big deal? It doesn't work out you just don't see him again." Sharona nodded, and said nothing. They'd been pushing her, Janet and Veronica and the new girl, Elaine, who was married and had two children. Janet wore a thick silver-coloured ring on her thumb. Her sweater hugged every lump and bump. Nothing hidden about her. Janet had had three boyfriends in the past six months and she was always talking about who liked what and who snored and who had morning breath.

Elaine brought in photos. With the help of their dad, her children had built a snowman. He was bigger than they were. His round bottom firm on the snow. Stick arms reaching left and right. Lopsided stone eyes. He'd be half-gone tomorrow, Sharona thought. The sun combined with people kicking at his melting base. Elaine pinned up the photos—the snowman, a birthday party, the boy and the girl smiling fiercely. The girl was missing her front teeth.

Sharona headed back to her cubby. Slipped off her shoes and curled her toes into the carpet, like a primate.

Raymond was on the news. A cluster of women stood around him waving signs. Sharona leaned toward the television, hand over her mouth. One woman pumped her fist in the air. "Remove the Sleepwalker!" She had a piercing on the side of her lower lip and she was talking about feeling threatened, about keeping the campus safe for all women. "It's an assault!" another woman said. "It's totally inappropriate. A trigger!" Raymond stood behind the protesters. His limbs lacked muscle tone and his belly bulged over the elastic of his underwear. There was snow on his bald head. Sharona turned off the television.

Janet coaxed Sharona to come to karaoke. "Might work for you," she whispered when they walked in. "Check it out." She was looking at two men thumbing their phones. Sharona didn't want to sing. She sipped wine, nodded, smiled, shook her head, smiled. No, no thank you. Not right now. And then Janet chose

THE NAKED MAN

"My Sharona" and the two men Janet had invited to sit with them said, *right on!* The older one, the one with rectangular glasses and spiky hair, put his hand on Sharona's thigh and drew circles with his index finger. Janet giggled. "Okay, guys, let's do this!" She touched the man beside her on his nose, pushed up her breasts, smoothed her jeans over her hips and walked to the stage. As she gyrated, she blew a kiss. And then she belted out the refrain, pumping her fist and her hips. The man with the rectangular glasses had his hand on his crotch, head nodding yes, yes, yes, in time to the beat. The other man sang along with his eyes closed. But Sharona bolted to the bathroom before the song had ended. She called a cab. Texted Janet that she was sorry.

On the weekend, the grounds at the College were empty and the snow was fresh, apart from discarded beer cans, two of which were stuck to the frozen grey mittens someone had pulled over Raymond's outstretched hands. Sharona pulled off the cans and removed the mittens, which she placed on the bench. His hands were brittle cold. She picked up the remaining cans that lay at Raymond's feet and set them in a tidy row beside the bench. She sat, opened a bag of Oreos and popped one whole into her mouth. Crumbs escaped, but Raymond didn't notice. She brushed them off her coat. "There's no Raymond song, at least there's that. But the beer cans. Why do they have to do that?" Sharona ate twelve Oreos and then she rolled the top of the bag tight and put it into her purse. She'd go now. She should go. She could see her breath.

But then three girls arrived. One pulled out her phone and stood facing Raymond, while the other two arranged themselves on either side of him. Sharona picked up her purse and the mittens and moved to stand in front of the photographer. She looked at Raymond. His fingers whispered against the lapels of her coat. She could see the pain in his face, the trouble behind his closed eyes. These *humiliations*.

Last week he'd been wearing a black cone bra. The day before yesterday he was covered in scarves and shawls, a Target bag hung on his arm and a green, pilled winter hat sat on his head. One morning he'd been wearing swim goggles.

"Do you mind?" one of the girls said, her lip curling. The posing girls had long shiny hair. One wore a fur-trimmed hat and the other wore purple fuzzy earmuffs. They pressed the lean lines of their hips against Raymond's smooth, hard underwear.

Sharona stroked the insides of his wrists. *Good-bye.*

The girls laughed. "Like, what the fuck?" Long hair flicked back with confidence.

Sharona added the mittens to the box of Raymond's clothing that sat in the entrance of her apartment. She had taken everything home, carefully smoothing creases, shaking off snow and lint and hair. Scarves, Hawaiian skirt, hats, towels, sunglasses.

Eleven years ago, Sharona's grad date sang bits of "My Sharona" in the front seat of his parents' Impala at 2:30 in the morning. His hands had gone under her dress and he'd reached up her back and undone her bra, which was brand new and smelled of the department store. He smelled like earwax and his hands were damp tea towels. Sharona had closed her eyes tight and felt the sweat glide from her armpits to her waist.

Rectangular glasses called. She answered the phone expecting a wrong number. "For the record, I had a good time," he said. Sharona wasn't sure she remembered what he looked like. "Granted, I think your friend was a little over the top with her singing, Sharon. But if you want to go again? Maybe? What do you think?" Sharona told him she had a fear of crowded spaces. Then she wondered if this was true. She sat at her kitchen counter, toes jammed under her feet. She could feel a cramp starting. "It's okay," he said. "Everybody's got something. My ex has eczema. No matter what, she can't get rid of it." Sharona thought about lungs closing under water. "I gotta go now," she said. "The milk's boiling over." She had trouble getting the words to loosen from her tongue.

On Tuesday a man sat beside her, just like that, out of the blue. He sat on the bench, crossed one leg over the other and folded his gloved hands on his lap. "Not bad out," he said, "considering it's January and all." His hair was sandy-coloured and longish over his ears. He shook his head, looking at Raymond. "Unbelievable. Just like he's real. Kind of amazing, you must admit." Sharona folded up the newspaper and took out her sandwich, which was egg salad.

She listened to another voicemail from the Indian man. "I called you the other day, but you have not returned my call. The squirrel, you see. I need…" And she'd missed another call. A woman with rats.

Sharona contacted the phone company to complain, but they told her there was nothing they could do. Unless she wanted a new number. "It's not our fault that folks dial wrong. I'm sorry, Ma'am." People called her Ma'am now. She asked Janet when that started and Janet rolled her eyes and said, "What you want to go for is *sexy*. Hold your voice in your throat. No offence."

Thursday she unwrapped a plain cheese sandwich. It was windy. She had trouble folding the wrap and finally balled it up and pushed it into her pocket. The sandy-haired man didn't show up.

And then a decision was made. They were moving him. Janet bubbled with it. "Finally!" she said, blinking her too-bright blue eyes. Janet wore mauve eye shadow and blue-black mascara and Sharona thought it was all a bit much, but then she wasn't sure. Sharona wore nothing but lip balm and only in the winter to alleviate the inevitable chapping. "They're hauling that thing off to a gallery. Can you imagine? I mean, where's the frigging imagination in a man who looks just like a man? Call that art? I could do that. Anyways, we're going for sushi. Coming? Also, I got a site for you to try. I even made you a profile. And what about Tony? Did he call? He said he was going to."

When the protesters had come into the HR office last week, everyone clustered around and then what could Sharona do? Janet thrust the pen at her. "You're gonna wanna sign, I mean, oh my god. It's for people like you that he's gotta go, Sharona. I mean, right? Have you even seen him? I can't walk that way anymore—have to go the long way round." She'd closed her eyes and shaken her head and everyone had sighed and shaken their heads with her. Perfume and shampoo scent wafted over Sharona. She held the pen over the petition for a count of ten before handing it back, her thumb over the line. Yes, she said, yes, they'd all be safer this way, and they looked at her and smiled and she'd felt their sympathy and recognized how awry sympathy could go.

Orange pylons dotted the snow. A man in a reflective vest waved his hand, urging on the flashing light and insistent beeps that were the truck backing up. Sharona sat on the bench near Raymond. The man in the vest had asked her to move, said it could be problematic, she might be in the way. But she hadn't moved. And he'd shrugged and left her. There was nobody but her. She'd been there since early morning. She'd brushed the snow off his shoulders and the top of his head, rubbed his whole body down with a towel. He was gleaming. Gleaming.

The workmen laid Raymond on his back in the truck. They tossed in the pylons, which landed dully. One bounced to rest against Raymond's belly. His bare arms and leading leg reached upward into the falling snow. He was smaller now, flat on his back.

"You have yourself a good day," the man called.

THE NAKED MAN

    She stayed on the bench and watched the truck disappear. She was wearing the scarf, the pilled hat, the grey mittens, and the Hawaiian skirt. Beside her was the Target bag filled with the rest of the discards. The snow kept coming. Record snowfalls this year, the weather lady had said yesterday. There was no end in sight.

At home Sharona sank into the cushions on her sofa. Closed her eyes. She imagined Raymond's arms stretching from one side of her tiny kitchen to the other. Where would they take him?
    The phone rang and she scrambled. "Hello?"
    "Finally. Yes. Why you are not returning my call?" It was the Indian man. His voice rose as he talked about violation and damage and noise. "They do not belong inside my house!"
    She couldn't disagree. She nodded, yes, yes.
    "You are listening? You are there? Who I am speaking to?" His *indignation.*
    "Sharona," she said. "My name is Sharona. Not Sharon. Sharona. Like the song."
    "I don't know Sharone, and I don't know any song. What kind of song it is?"
    She saw herself in the black television screen. "I work at the College," she said. "They've removed the naked man. Today. They did it today." She smoothed her hair, which was sticking up. But when she lifted her hand the hair rose with it.
    The man exhaled hard into the phone. "They are everywhere," he said.
    Sharona licked her palm and patted her head carefully to settle the wayward strands.

RUTHIE

RUTHIE MCLEAN EXAMINES HER FACE IN THE CAMPER mirror. She holds her chin high, stretches her throat taut, and looks for worry lines, dry skin, crow's feet. The signs of decline. She's thirty-six years old and she looks tired. Of course she does—four kids, a husband who works shifts, the mortgage, the endless bills, the neighbour who complains about noise. But her eyes are bright, her teeth and nose are straight, her hair is silky waves. Still. She could end up in a car accident or some other kind of accident that puts an end to all of it. She could get an incurable illness. You have to take advantage, that's what she thinks. She doesn't want to be one of those people who drifts through life. Wastes it.

She opens her brand-new tube of burgundy-red lipstick and applies it carefully. Blots and reapplies. The thing is, she thinks, you don't want to end up dying, wishing you'd done something to make your heart sit up and take notice. Something dangerous. The lipstick is perfect. Rich and deep. A kind of promise. Things are going to happen! that's what the colour says. She pokes her head out of the bathroom door and looks at Don, who is sprawled across the bed in the back. It's almost three, and as soon as he wakes up, they'll get going. As soon as. She checks her reflection again, pulls her mouth into a pout, blows a kiss, and whispers, "Let's go, Ruthie." And then she opens the camper door.

RUTHIE

They've made it. Finally. She can almost smell it, almost taste it—the Stampede. The Greatest Outdoor Show on Earth. She touches her hair, and then, in her crisp, sleeveless white blouse, her flounce skirt, and the purple cowboy boots she found at the thrift store, she steps outside to wait with the kids in the gravel lot that is their campsite.

It's hot. The kids look at her expectantly. "I know," she whispers, finger on her lips. "I know. Real soon, okay?"

Even though none of it is easy, even though she feels like killing them sometimes, she's proud of them. They're seven, five, four, and two-and-a-half. Molly and Eva are in the short-sets Ruthie bought at Walmart. Molly's is blue with red trim and Eva's red with blue trim. The boys are in denim shorts and matching T-shirts. Cam is the oldest, tall and responsible, and Buddy is the pudgy baby. They have the same serious brown eyes, the same solid temperaments—her bookends she calls them. "Tell you what," she says. "Let's line up. Get you all polished." She wipes their hands and faces with Wet Ones, redoes Molly's braids, pulling the hair tight and tighter, re-clips little Eva's barrettes so they won't slip. "We've got to be ready for when Daddy wakes up." She uses spit to slick down Buddy's flyaway hair.

"Why can't we play exploring? Why can't we do that?" Molly stands with hands on her hips, defiant. She's almost as tall as Cam, who says, "Yeah. Why can't we do something?"

"Because we're going to the Stampede," Ruthie says. "That's why. And we're staying here two whole nights. Don't forget how lucky you are." The hushed voice because Don worked all night and then did the long drive. "Give me a break, Ruthie," he'd said when she complained that they'd been in the camper all day, that they were dressed up and ready. "The Stampede will still be there when I wake up." At five in the morning when he got home from work, instead of coming to bed, he'd gone and changed the oil in the camper van. Of course it needed doing, she got that, but why couldn't he have done it the day before? Why hadn't he thought of that?

There's no shade in the wide-open campsite. And there's nothing to do. The sparseness of it—no trees, no forest smells, traffic just a bit farther up. Far as Ruthie can tell, the whole place is nothing more than a couple of abandoned lots, a makeshift space to accommodate the campers who've arrived for the Stampede. "All right. Okay then," she says and she takes Molly and Buddy by the hand, tells Cam not to let go of Eva and to stay close. "We'll have a look at the place. But we don't have a whole lot of time." Because how long can Don sleep?

They find the taps and the garbage bins, the waste hook-up and the power hook-up. Cam wants to run and Ruthie hisses for him to behave. "Right now!" Eva whines that Cam's pulling. "Cam! I'm telling you…" She squeezes Molly and Buddy's hands too tight. She's hot. And her hair's going flat, she can feel it.

Two couples, heavyset men and women, with red faces, cowboy hats and jeans, sit in lawn chairs in front of a huge silver domed camper that blinks in the sunlight. They're drinking beer. One man takes his feet off a double-size cooler to look Ruthie up and down. "Hot enough for ya?"

Ruthie doesn't smile. She doesn't respond. To Molly she hisses, "Don't let me get like that." Molly stares and sticks her finger in her mouth. Ruthie smacks it away.

When she and Don talked about a camper Ruthie pictured something shiny and brand new. She imagined it would be well appointed in an IKEA kind of way with a perfect spot for everything. Instead, Don brought home an old camper van, dull yellow, rusting around the bumpers. An eyesore. "They didn't look like that," she said. The brochures were stacked in a tidy pile beside her bed. She'd pored over them for weeks. Pointed out features to Don—hardwood floors, captain seats, granite countertops. Toilets and showers that looked like real toilets and showers.

"The engine's good," Don said. "Rock solid these old Fords. They don't build 'em like this anymore. And no loan, Ruthie. She's ours. That counts for a lot."

RUTHIE

Ruthie opened the little cupboard doors and the drawers, opened and closed them. She stopped herself from going on about the smell and the torn upholstery. Didn't say anything when he showed her the way the benches and table folded into a bed that was too short for anyone who wasn't short. She made covers for the seat cushions and hung new curtains on the plastic rods. She scrubbed every inch of everything with bleach and then sprayed lemon air freshener and put a mat at the entrance. The musty smell lingered but it wasn't as obvious.

They'd left right after the breakfast clean-up, which took longer than it should've because Buddy pooped on the floor before Ruthie'd had a chance to put him on the potty or into a diaper. Don told her not to worry, they had loads of time. "It's a holiday," he said, "not a race." She packed crayons and books and stickers and snacks, got everyone dressed and into the camper, fretted about forgetting something as obvious as the tickets for the fireworks and the Grandstand show. And the first hour in the camper had gone well. The kids drew and stickered and were excited about all of it. Ruthie leaned back against her seat and closed her eyes. She thought about the way her skirt flitted above her knees, how her knees were smooth and how her shoulders were rounded soft and lightly browned. She thought about the people who'd be all around, the excitement. She'd been to the Stampede before—she'd been thirteen—her brother begging for donuts and to see the animals, her parents anxious about cost and time. Ruthie had watched boys drape their arms over girls' shoulders, girls press their breasts against the boys' arms. She'd stood apart from her family, shrugged her tank strap loose, bared her shoulder, and felt the thrum of the boys' energy sweep over her. And then her dad had the donuts. Her mom called again. "Ruthie!" She'd followed her parents and her brother to the Agriculture building, but every inch of her ached to stay with the boys whose eyes burned her.

It should have been a four-and-a-half-hour drive, but that didn't take into account the construction delays on the road, the stops for the bathroom and gas, and the picnic lunch at the side of the highway. The kids grew tired of the crayons. The stickers were finished. Eva whined that Molly had pinched her. Molly said Eva pinched first. She thumped Eva on the head with the colouring book. Cam wouldn't read *The Cat in the Hat* to Buddy. He looked out the window at endless rolling prairie and said he had a tummy ache. So Ruthie undid her seat belt and climbed into the back. She squeezed between the girls, read and reread whatever book they handed her until Buddy fell asleep. She told herself it was going to be worth it. They were going to have a good time.

There's nothing to see. The campground is duller than dull. There's a river, but you have to cross two roads to get to it. Cam says why can't they do that? He wants to go to the river, he's *boiling!* Ruthie reminds him that they came all this way to see the Stampede not some stupid river that'll be just like every other stupid river in the stupid world. "Anyways," she says, "Daddy's gonna be up now so we don't have time for any rivers."

A shuttle bus pulls up alongside the water taps. Ruthie sees the fat cowboy-hat people file on. The bus is going to the Stampede. Taking them there.

"Wait one sec!" she tells the kids.

She ignores their questions, crosses the dirt track, and climbs onto the bus behind Hot-Enough-For-Ya, who winks and says, "Ready to party?"

Ruthie smiles, a little. She can't help it. She *is* ready. And then she asks the driver, "What time are you leaving because... Can you wait for just a bit? We're almost ready."

The driver's cowboy hat is tipped back. "You getting on?" His face is round and without expression.

"Well, I want to but..." She glances at the kids in the distance—they're standing close together, eyes on the bus—and then in the direction of the camper van. "We're just about ready. It's my husband... Can you wait? Just a couple minutes?"

The driver looks into his rear-view. "I got a schedule, ma'am."

The camper door is still closed. Ruthie sees that the drawn curtains look all wrong from outside, too stark, too new against the dull paint. Buddy drops to the ground and sits with legs splayed. He picks up a handful of gravel and tosses it, again, again. Molly whispers something to Eva and both of them look first at Ruthie and then toward the edge of the campsite. Cam leans over the firepit and blows on the ashes.

Ruthie drags the yellow nylon fold-up chair to the middle of the site and sits down to wait. Her whole body is ready. The lipstick. The blouse, the skirt. She looks at her feet. Turns them side to side. The cowboy boots pinch and they're hot. But they're beautiful.

"Can we make a fire?" Cam asks.

"No, we can't."

"Why not? Why can't we?"

"Because. Because we're not doing that."

"How come?"

And then she shakes her head. "Okay." She throws up her hands. "You know what? You get us some wood then. You and Buddy. Go. Go get the wood. Go right ahead." She watches them walk away, Buddy's hand in Cam's.

"Mom?" Molly calls. "We're gonna play Snow White and you hafta be the step-lady."

Ruthie doesn't respond. All Molly ever wants is make-believe everything. If she had her way the living room would be a permanent Arabian tent, sheets and blankets over the furniture, her bedroom ceiling would be stars and moons. They'd all be dressed as queens and princesses.

"And after, you be the mean witch and I'll be Snow White and Eva's gonna be the prince."

"We're going to the Stampede, Molly. That's fun. That's *real* fun. There's candy. And rides. And the fireworks, remember? People go to the Stampede to have fun. Lots of people."

"I don't wanna Stampede. I wanna stay here."

Ruthie ignores her. She stares into the firepit. They will have a fire. They'll have it when they get back. It'll be dark and they'll toast marshmallows before bed. She and Don will have a drink and he'll say what a great time they had. The kids will be asleep, exhausted and happy, and he'll put his hand on her knee; he'll pull off her cowboy boots one at a time. The lust. That's the thing she misses. It covered everything.

The girls drift away. They go to the other side of the site to poke around in the thin shrubs and tall grass that borders the gravel. Ruthie watches them pile up leaves and twigs and stones into some kind of Molly-order. It doesn't take much for them to be distracted. She closes her eyes. It's just so darn hot. And now it's almost 4:30. She told Don they had to make a full day of it and he said he got that. Obviously, he said. But what did that mean?

Buddy puts a hot hand on her arm. Ruthie starts, opens her eyes. Was she asleep? The boys are back. Cam has dropped three small logs beside the firepit and now he's holding a stick and the girls are beside him; they have sticks, too. And then Buddy leaves her side to pick up a fourth stick, and all of them poke the ashes, stir and flick and make grey, fine dust fly up to settle onto their clothes and skin.

"Watch this, Mom," Cam shouts. "Tornado!"

"Aw, Cam! For crying out loud!" She waves her arms to keep the dust away. "You're getting it everywhere!"

She can't be falling asleep like that. Don will wake up and they'll all be waiting for her because she'll be the one sleeping. In the fold-up chair. She sits up a bit, focuses on watching the kids play. It's okay. It's fine. There's still time, she tells herself. Four-thirty, five o'clock, it's not too late. And Buddy had a nap so he won't be cranky during the fireworks

RUTHIE

and the show. They're having dinner at the Stampede. Hot dogs or corn dogs, cotton candy. She lets her eyes fall shut again. The kids aren't being noisy and they're not whining or fighting. Oh, but she's parched! At the Stampede they'll have slushies and snow cones. The music and fanfare, the smell of grease and stickiness and horses, the warm bodies. They'll go on the chair ride first, the one that takes you across the entire grounds so you can see all the places you'll go. And she's going to get them each their own strip of tickets and let them choose whichever ride they want and maybe let them try the games, maybe they'll win a prize, maybe Don will shoot for her and win one of those huge stuffed toys that you can barely hold onto and she and the kids will be so proud of him and he'll be proud too, although he'll walk on with a frown as though he doesn't care even though she knows he does.

She has to stay awake. Heavy eyes that don't really want to open anymore. Around the firepit the kids have grown hazy, their voices are background noise. Her armpits are damp and she lifts her elbows to let air in. She hears murmurs and squeals, a siren far off, a lawn mower or a chainsaw. Don uses a chainsaw sometimes. A motor home starts up—someone is leaving. They've seen everything and now they're heading back to Saskatoon or down south somewhere. She doesn't want to be too late. When you're late all the good stuff's gone, the shine's worn off. Shine of her boots, her hair, her lipstick. She shifts in the lawn chair, feels the swell of her breasts inside her blouse, the swell of her body. She presses her fingertips against the insides of her thighs. The heat! Somewhere, she hears Eva. Hears Eva and feels beads of sweat trickle a wet line between her breasts.

The shrill cry.

Eyes open. It takes her a moment. A cry? Is this the second cry? The third? Eva! How long has Eva been crying?

Molly is holding a stick straight up in the air like a flagpole and Ruthie lunges.

Without thinking, without registering who is hurt, what is hurt, how bad anything is, she snatches the stick and whips—whack! whack! whack!—across the back of Molly's legs, cries out, "What *happened*? What are you *doing!*" Blinking to focus in the glare of the sun, blinking and blinking to see the blood on Eva's face and hands, seeping out from between her fingers, trickling down her wrists. She pulls at Eva's hands, shouts for the kids to not just stand there! "Get Daddy! Can't you see that you should get Daddy?"

Eva sinks onto the ground and Ruthie sees that the shortset is ruined. Dust and blood smeared together on the clean pattern—they can't go to the Stampede like this. "Don! *Don-ny!*"

Of course he's heard them. Of course they've woken him. She sees him at the door of the camper, adjusting his pants, squinting into the sunlight, his hair sticking up, face pressed with bed wrinkles.

"You were sleeping!" she shouts. Before he can ask what's going on, what she was doing.

He flies down the step, across the gravel. Drops to the ground and scoops Eva into his arms. "A towel, Ruthie! A cloth. Something! Something clean. And hurry!"

She hurries. But it isn't easy to find things in the camper. It's too small, too tight, there's no air. "Molly!" Where are the towels? Cloths? They're here just two days, she doesn't have... She wipes sweaty hands on the bottom of her skirt, rifles through the jumble of diapers, extra clothes, juice boxes, crayons, books, blankets, shirts, crackers, plastic bags spread on the table and benches, the Rubbermaid tote on the floor, the cooler. "Molly!" She can't find anything. Where's Molly!

"Mom?"

"I can't find..." Then, in the pocket of the diaper bag, finally, the box of Band-Aids. Of course. She always carries them. In case of minor emergencies. She stumbles to the camper door, lurches down the step, the box in front of her. "It's okay, Don! I've got it!"

RUTHIE

He looks at the box in her hands, looks at her. "Band-Aids! I don't need fucking Band-Aids! Get me a cloth, Ruthie! I've got to stop the bleeding! Christ! She's going to lose her eye!"

But Molly is already there. A folded diaper in her hand. She gives it to Don and he opens it and presses it flat so that it covers most of Eva's face. Don is focussed on Eva, who is whimpering now, no longer crying. He doesn't look at Ruthie.

She holds the box of Band-Aids against her chest and just for a second she's almost laughing. Or crying. She doesn't know. Don and his seriousness, the blood and the mess of everything. Appalled at her uselessness, ashamed of even her presence, holding onto the ridiculous little box. She sees the welts rising on the backs of Molly's legs, her face wet and streaked with dust.

Don drives the camper van. The map is open on his lap and he tells Ruthie don't worry about it, he can figure out how to get there, tells her to concentrate on holding Eva, which she does. The kids sit tight together on the bench seat.

"There was no fire, Don. I didn't let them build a fire," Ruthie says. "I told them they had to wait. Until you got up."

"You don't let three-year-olds play with sticks. Everyone knows that."

She sees the shake of his head, almost imperceptible, tight and grim. It's not just Eva. She knows that. "She's four," she whispers.

"What?"

"Nothing. I didn't say anything." She breathes in Eva's smell, holds her close, holds the diaper in place.

At the hospital they wait. They sit in the emergency beside whining kids and old people with their heads down, people with tubes attached, people who look fine and people who are crying in pain and are bleeding but not badly enough to be rushed in. They bribe and cajole the kids to behave; they take turns walking around outside with them, buying them Popsicles and counting red cars in the parking lot. And then the doctor stitches Eva's eyebrow and eyelid. Three times he asks them how it happened, and Ruthie can't answer, can't look at him. "Kids will be kids," Don says again. The eye will be swollen and turn blue and black, the doctor says, but it's going to be fine.

Don carries Eva back through the waiting room where the seats are still filled. Ruthie follows with the kids. She doesn't look at the people. Her lips are chapped and her blouse is sticking to her chest and back. Her boots are too loud on the linoleum floor.

Once they're back in the camper, Ruthie remembers the Stampede. All that time in the hospital she didn't think about it, and now she does. It's 7:30 and it's still light out. She's surprised somehow. Surprised at the brightness, surprised to see the partygoers on the streets, young people shouting and yahooing and making their way to the Stampede grounds. Don starts whistling a children's song and at first Ruthie doesn't recognize the tune, but then she does. *All around the mulberry bush, the monkey chased the weasel.* That he's whistling, this surprises her, too. A waking dream, she thinks, that's what it is.

And then she says, "Maybe we could still make it. We have the tickets and all. I mean…" She twists to look at the kids, at little Eva, drugged and asleep, taking up the entire second bench. "It wouldn't have happened if… If we'd been at the Stampede. If you'd been up. We'd be there now."

Don stops whistling. "It did happen, Ruthie. You were there." And then he says, "Why don't you go? You could catch the fireworks."

Ruthie wraps her arms around herself. Her toes have gone numb inside the purple boots. She feels Don's eyes on her and she sees the explosions, the startling bursts of colour, the way everything disappears in an instant.

VOICE LESSONS

THE SINGING LESSONS ARE A KIND OF PHYSICAL THERAPY, Mylene explains. "I'm doing it to open my vocal cords," she whispers. "Not because I want to be a singer." She wants Barbara Kroondijk to understand that it's not an exercise in self-indulgence. It's not a whim. She keeps her eyes on the table, nervous. Shy really. Because even though Barbara Kroondijk is no longer part of her life, Mylene is concerned about what she might think and anxious that she should empathize. Mostly, she's afraid of her judgement. It's laughable, this fear, but she can't smother it. "I tried other ways," she says. "I did three sessions of massage—the doctor's hands on my throat for an hour each time. It works for some people. That's what they say. Apparently."

"Well, good for you," Barbara says. "Fingers crossed for a miracle. Pay your money, take your chances kind of thing." She's still wearing her apron and one hand rests on her order pad. She speaks as though she's not really listening. As though her mind is still on the coffee shop and her customers, or the cook, who went home an hour ago.

"It's supposed to be effective," Mylene says. "And." She pauses. She doesn't want to sound defensive. Or pushy. But. "You can't really call it a miracle. It's more like you with piano, you know? The music? That's why I'm telling you. Because you get it. You know what I'm talking about. The power of music. You always got that. You know?"

Barbara drums the table with her nails. "My guy shouldn't be too long," she says. Her hands are old and work-worn, but the nails are young—thick and long and gleaming vibrant-red. They click plastic. "How 'bout a beer while we wait?"

Mylene tucks her own clipped nails into her palms and shakes her head. "Hopefully I'll be driving soon. You know. So, no thanks. But thanks. You still play?"

Barbara doesn't answer. She heads to the kitchen, leaving Mylene alone at her window seat where she's spent the entire day waiting for the garage mechanic to fix her car. It's sitting at the pumps. Exactly where she left it. She'd been on her way home from the Badlands where she spent the weekend at her first-ever vocal conference. She stopped for gas and then couldn't restart her car. That's what got her stuck here.

The gas station is next door to the coffee shop. Separated by an empty lot. Gravel and broken asphalt strewn with discarded tires, decomposing cardboard, rotting mattresses, rusted vehicle parts. There's the occasional stalwart shrub or clump of dandelions pushing through the debris. Some things survive no matter what, Mylene thinks. A forgotten billboard stands tall, its message spent or forgotten or no longer significant. JES-- -S --- --SWE-. The image that accompanied the words is faded to almost nothing and most of that has peeled off. Jessie is sweet, Mylene thinks. Imagining the delight of a little girl with a billboard dedicated to her.

The scattered buildings that make up a small town are a little farther along the highway. She thought about walking there this morning, but then didn't, certain that at any moment the mechanic would walk in and pronounce her car fixed.

Last night, instead of the wine and cheese wrap-up, she walked to the dinosaur museum and wandered among reconstructed skeletons, fake sand dunes, displays of massive femurs, rib cages, jaw bones. The voice teacher, Mary-Beth Porczak, who was slight and sharp, more ballerina than soprano, her body as precise as crystal, told Mylene to visualize a tunnel, dark and wide. A tunnel through which sound could move as smoothly and efficiently as water in a concrete channel. According to Mary-Beth, releasing sound was similar to birthing. The same harnessing of mind power to manipulate the body. In the museum's impressive expanse, Mylene thought about this harnessing of power as she wandered past the Albertosaurus and the Tyrannosaurus Rex, the Triceratops and the Camarasaurus. She sounded out the names in her head. Recorded birdsong accompanied her. She'd never given birth. That was the thing.

"My voice is nothing to worry about," she'd whispered to her husband when they first met. She was used to it, she told him; she knew no different. It had been a problem when she was younger, she said, but not now. Vocal clarity, the clear, resonant, *normal* sounds one expects with speech, are trapped deep in her throat cavity by larynx muscles that won't cooperate. Andy told her he didn't mind. There was nothing wrong with gentle and soft-spoken, and he liked leaning in to hear what she had to say. "Lucky it's you and not me," he said. Meaning that for a male it might be worse. It's because of Andy that she's here. Since he's lost his job he wanders through the house in a T-shirt and underwear, unshaven and purposeless.

Across the lot the car looks desolate. The key is stuck. It won't turn and it can't be removed. He'd see what he could do, the owner-mechanic said. He'd get to it as soon as possible. And then half an hour ago, he handed Mylene a card and said it looked like she'd have to wait until tomorrow. She'd texted Andy on the verge of tears. And then Barbara came to her assistance. "Tell you what," she said. "I got a guy. He'll get you outta here in no time." She plunked a serving of apple pie on the table. "Complimentary," she said and winked. "I'm just closing up. Stay right here. One more minute." So Mylene relaxed. She watched Barbara deal with the stragglers and remembered the piano playing. Carnegie Hall had been Barbie Kroondijk's singular ambition. But here she was. In a small-town coffee shop a half-hour's drive from the slightly larger and moderately prettier small town in which they'd grown up. With the taste of apple pie on her tongue, Mylene felt lighter, happier. Because didn't that wink signal a level of complicity? The trip hadn't been a waste of time; something good would come of it. That's what she thought.

She hadn't recognized Barbara at first. She'd been mildly aware that there was something familiar about the waitress, who was big and brassy, loud and ebullient, full of life. A woman who enjoyed herself a little too much, Mylene thought. Or too *forcefully*. The way she tilted her head, the way she laughed, the slight motion in her hip and shoulders that acted as punctuation when she spoke. The tease in her voice that was friendly and at the same time verged on offensive. But it was the eyes that gave her away—pale blue with whites visible around the entire irises—Mylene was sure she recognized them. This was her sister's best friend from primary school. Barbie Kroondijk. When the waitress came to the table the next time, making her rounds, coffee pot hovering, her face a question, Mylene smiled tentatively and whispered, "Barbie?"

The response was curt, almost unfriendly. "Do I look like a Barbie? It's Barbara." She tapped her nametag. "Barbara."

For a second Mylene was confused, unsure whether she'd actually recognized her or made a mistake. "Do you remember Annie?" she whispered. "Your friend?"

"Huh?"

Mylene focussed on relaxing her throat, willing neurons to engage with larynx muscles and diaphragm. She was acutely aware that whispering could be taken as a slight, as impertinence or rudeness, so she looked away, taking her time as she'd been taught, and tried hard to visualize the open channel before she attempted to speak. "Aa—"

"You okay? You had enough? Or you want the menu again?"

"Aa-nnie." It came out solid. Slightly too solid, so that it landed annoyed. "Do you remember?"

And then Barbara nodded. "Oh yeah, yeah. Annie. Wait. You mean *Annie*-Annie? You're *Annie*? Gawwwd!"

Mylene shook her head, hand on her chest in a kind of apology. "No, no, no, no," she whispered. "Not me. My sister. She's Annie. I'm Mylene. Mylene McCormick."

"Okay, okay. Yeah, sure." Her eyes didn't stay on Mylene and her look was slightly ambiguous so that Mylene wasn't sure. But the shop was busy. Barbara was scanning the room for cups to fill, orders to take. She had a job to do. Couldn't be chatting too long. And in any case, she'd always been odd. A wild card, frenetic and unpredictable. Someone to be afraid of. Mylene's mother had never liked her. She couldn't understand what Annie and Mylene saw in her. Five-year-old Mylene had said she loved her, she wanted to marry her. Barbie and Annie were inseparable at school, complaining to the principal if they weren't in the same class, to the teacher if their seats weren't side by side. They dressed the same, had identical haircuts. And when Barbie was at their house, Annie ignored her voiceless younger sister. Barbie had long, shimmering hair. And those eyes! They frightened even as they beckoned. She tickled Mylene until she threw up, pinched her until she cried, stole her candy, hid her toys, ripped her books. But no matter what she did, Mylene wanted more. Barbie said Mylene was beautiful, told her to rub her perfect skin against the soft pink insulation around the pipe in the school bathroom. Which Mylene did.

There's a competence about grown-up Barbara, Mylene thinks as she waits for her to return from the kitchen. Everyone who came into the shop knew her, and she knew them. Or, if she didn't, if they were tourists on their way to or from the hoodoos or the dinosaur museum or the buffalo jump, she might as well have known them, she was that familiar. Even as a child Barbie had that magnetic self-assurance. Mylene remembers it. The allure. And she remembers that Barbie Kroondijk pushed her into the creek where she almost drowned.

Barbara has been gone a long time, Mylene realizes suddenly. Is it that she's annoyed? Regretting her offer of help and companionship? Wishing Mylene wasn't here? But no—she does come back. She's taken off her apron, changed into jeans and a sweatshirt and she's carrying a six-pack. "Sure you don't want one?" She holds out a can.

"I'm okay."

Barbara drinks steadily, finishing one beer and cracking the next while Mylene goes on with her explanation about the conference and the singing, about her desire, her *hope*, to be cured of her affliction. It's unsettling to realize that despite the weekend's work, she's still whispering. "It takes time to learn," she says. "The technique. That's what they told us. And everything takes time, right? I mean, look at my car!"

"His name's Isaac," Barbara says, putting her can down hard. "He can fix anything with nothing. Forget about those parts that John asshole is saying you need. He's blowing smoke. Him and his old lady run a B&B and this is what he does. Gave you his card, right?"

The card shows a white picket fence, lush trees and the glimmer of a red metal roof. "Reasonable rates" is written in italics and followed by two exclamation marks.

"Isaac? He'll have you home before dark, guaranteed. Make your hubby happy. Sorry. Is there a hubby? Or...?"

"Yeah. There is. Andy. We've been married fifteen years. You?"

"Nope. You guys have kids too? The whole thing?"

"No," Mylene says. "No kids. It wasn't in the cards for us, I guess. I'm not maternal, maybe. And Andy, too. I mean. You know. My husband." She pauses, glancing at Barbara. She can feel the significance of what she's about to say pressing against her breastbone—her core saying stop even as her mouth keeps going. "I'm here because of him. That's why I came. Because the thing is—my husband? Andy? He's unemployed. Let go, so to speak. And—I've sort of lost confidence. You know what I mean? In him. I mean, he's… I don't know. He's…" She shakes her head. "It's that all of a sudden I *need* to do this. The voice lessons. I'm angry at him, I guess. Annoyed. Or impatient. And I want to *show* him. Something." And then she adds, "I said it was a work thing. The conference. That's what I told him." It's that every day his soul sinks deeper into a pit. His limbs are shrinking, his skin thinning. He no longer picks up his feet when he walks. "I can't explain it," she says and she can hear the plea in her words. This is the first time she's voiced her frustration.

Barbara closes her eyes. Her shoulders are rounder, her head heavier. "I remember," she says slowly. And Mylene takes a deep breath. She feels a weight begin to lift. The beer is loosening Barbara's tongue. Mylene is going to hear something nice. Barbie Kroondijk is going to smile and say, don't worry about it, I get what you're saying, I understand. And then she's going to apologize—gently, *genuinely*—for everything that happened all those years and years ago. The creek. The bullying. The taking advantage of a child's idolization. It's not necessary, Mylene will tell her. It's okay. And she'll smile. They'll hug. Cry, maybe.

She wants a drink now. She does. "Wait," she whispers, lifting her hand. "Hold that thought. Sorry, but—do you have wine by chance? Sorry. To bother you and all. But before you go on—maybe I'd have a glass. Just one. You know—to take the edge off. It's been a long day, right? I figure I deserve it. If you have any, that is."

Barbara says sure, yeah, no problem. She pushes up from the table and heads to the kitchen.

The intimacy of sharing a drink, opening up, apologizing together, this is what Mylene wants. It's as though fate has brought her here. To Barbara Kroondijk's cafe. Wow. She can actually feel her voice box opening, actually feel, physically, what it would be like to belt out a song right now.

Barbara comes back carrying a coffee cup and a bottle of white. She pours the wine into two water glasses.

"You work here every day?"

"Yep. Pretty much." Barbara holds up the coffee cup. "Ice?"

"No thanks," Mylene says. "I'm fine." And then, raising her glass, "To seeing you again."

"I remember you," Barbara says. She chases the first mouthful of wine with a swig of beer. "The whole whisper thing. Cracks me up just hearing you. Still the same. Like you're trying to be a lover or something. Even back then. I mean honestly, right? Pretty weird stuff."

Mylene takes several sips of the warm wine in rapid succession. "In a million years," she says, "I never thought you'd be in a place like this. Don't get me wrong—it's nice. But still. The piano. The music. That was your thing." She finishes her glass. Generosity, that's what this is about.

Barbara doesn't answer and Mylene feels badly right away. "I'm not judging you," she says. "Things change, right?" She adds a laugh, a quick burst of air, barely more than silence. "And you look great. Really. As always. Plus, the way you handle the people here. I've been watching you. All day. It's amazing. Honestly." She's five again, from top to bottom. Five and vulnerable. Five and impressionable. She's going to say that she wishes she worked in a coffee shop, not an accounting firm. That she thinks Barbara is wonderful. She's going to say she loved her, *still* loves her, she can feel it. And more. She can't stop herself. She's going to confess that the workshop didn't help, that she's afraid, that she's trying, *trying* to be strong, but that it's impossible. Doesn't Barbara feel the same way? Honestly? That the piano playing was all for nothing? That she's in this dump? She can feel the words, the emotion, swelling up in her.

Barbara settles low in her chair. "I remember driving once," she says. "With my mom. I can't remember where we were going, but there was something about it that felt like a huge promise, like it was something I'd been waiting a long time for, you know what I mean?"

Mylene nods and pours herself a second glass of wine, a small one. "I totally get that because I—" But Barbara keeps talking. Right over Mylene's whisper.

"When suddenly, there was this deer. It jumped out of the ditch—in my mind it's like this huge leap, magical, that big. Anyhow, this deer comes at us—flying, literally flying—and I think my mom brakes, she must have, or she screams or I scream or we both do. And then bam! we hit the deer. Like, obviously we hit it. But it's gone. Like that." She snaps her fingers. "Huge dent in the front of the car and this crack right across the entire windshield, but the frigging deer is gone. It was unbelievable. Me and my mom shitting ourselves, and then thinking we'd imagined it. Because we stopped, right? We had to see if it was dead. Can't just leave it, Mom said. We got out and looked around. But it was nowhere. Crazy. Totally crazy."

"But. Where were you going? What were you going to do?" Because surely that's the point of the story. The huge promise.

"So then later… Oh. I don't know. The deer thing has pretty much obliterated everything. Anyway. We come driving back that way after we did whatever we did and Mom slows where we hit the thing, but again we see nothing. So whatever. We go home.

"And then. It's three days, three days later and we're on the highway again and boom! This head comes up in the grass. It's the frigging deer. Like, oh my god! It's been lying there in the grass, almost dead, for three days. Yeah, right? Unbelievable. Maybe you think it's another deer, but no, we're positive that's where we hit it. So we get out of the car. Walk over, and it kind of flinches, but it can't move, and then it just puts its head down. Gives up. Blinking its eyes. So, yeah. We call the wildlife guy and he comes and shoots it and all that. But whoa, right? Pretty messed up."

She taps the table steadily with her bright fingernails and takes sips as she talks, alternating wine and beer indiscriminately. Every once in a while she tucks a strand of hair behind her ears, which are pierced up the cartilage with alternating blues and crystals. Seven bright studs in one and four in the other. She used to have a chin. Her waist has disappeared into her hips. Her eyes are the only thing that hasn't changed. They're enhanced with blue eye shadow and blue eyeliner. Everything about her is crass and tacky—the way she talks, the way she gestures. Mylene should be feeling superior, but instead she feels an urge so primal it can't be supplanted. She wants Barbie's hand on hers. She wants to be told that everything is okay.

Barbara is looking at her, slightly glassy-eyed. Doe-like, Mylene thinks, and she whispers, "That's pretty sad."

"Sad? That's just life, right? Shit happens, what are you gonna do? You pick yourself up and you move on. Except in the deer's case. Then you don't."

"But. Why are you telling me this? I mean."

"I don't know. Something about you."

A horrible unease settles in Mylene's belly. She wants to ask, wants to say something. But the door opens, the little bell startling her because the combination of the wine and the story has made her forget where they are.

The man who comes in is tall and broad-shouldered, with a pale face, cropped hair and a tidy beard. He's wearing old-fashioned waist-high black pants, black shoes, a sturdy-looking work shirt and suspenders.

The incongruity of him, Mylene thinks. Like he belongs and doesn't belong at the same time. A living relic.

Barbara gets up, smiling, listing, so that she has to catch herself on the back of the chair. "Isaac!"

The man nods.

"Isaac," Barbara says again. She seems nervous, oddly deferential, and also happy. But not with the joviality of before.

This is deeper. Emotional, somehow. The alcohol, Mylene thinks. She feels it too.

"Thanks so much," Barbara says. "I'm sorry to call when you've got Sarah and everything. But this is Mylene. She's got the car. You know. The lady with the car." She presses her lips together and lifts her eyebrows at Mylene so she knows to get up.

A shift has occurred without Mylene knowing why. There's a calmness about Isaac, a kind of unassuming strength, which he carries naturally and easily, but it's Barbara. Her attentiveness. It makes Mylene uncomfortable. As though something is her fault, as though she's interfering somehow.

They follow Isaac outside, where the air is stiller and the debris in the empty lot is holding fast to the concentrated colour of day's end. Mylene sees the dandelions, not yet closed, sharp as sunshine, the shining blacks and greys of the rubbish, the gleam of aluminium, everything heightened. Even the billboard is vibrant.

Isaac is already at the car, already reaching in, leaning across the seat, twisting to look at the stuck key. "*Ja*," he says. "I seen this sort of thing. This model. Old one, *ja*? Ten, twelve years?"

"I guess so," Mylene says. "Maybe ten. I'm not actually sure."

Barbara watches Isaac work, and then to his back she says, "Sarah all right?"

"*Ja*. Fine. Real good."

"The baby?"

"*Ja*. Good. He is the Lord's blessing."

Barbara nods. She keeps nodding, arms tight around her middle, and Mylene thinks she wants something further, more information maybe, details. Or she wants Isaac to turn around. But she doesn't say anything more and Isaac doesn't pause, doesn't look up. He shifts closer to the wheel, so that he's almost under the dash, shining his flashlight this way and that, pulling screwdrivers or wrenches out of the tool kit he set on the passenger seat. Barbara must have told him the problem, told him what to bring. Because he doesn't ask about anything; he just works. And after twenty or thirty minutes as the brightness of the sun's last hurrah is giving way to dusk, he's finished. He gets out of the car and presents Mylene with the freed key. "So," he says. "I think she's working now."

"I'm so grateful," she whispers. "I thought I'd never get out of here. I thought I was stuck here forever." She laughs a hoarse sound.

"Pardon?"

"It's her voice," Barbara says. "She has a defect." She puts her hand over her throat. "Sometimes nothing comes out, but mostly she's misunderstood. A kind of problem, see. Disability."

Isaac nods. He takes money that Barbara hands him so subtly Mylene doesn't realize it until later, at which point she questions Barbara, angry, and humiliated in a way that feels hopelessly familiar. By then Isaac is gone. He said no thank you to Barbara's offer of pie, coffee, anything. Got in his truck and drove off. She and Barbara are back in the coffee shop where Barbara is leaning against the counter, drinking the last of the beer.

"It's my voice!" Mylene says. "You don't have to go around making apologies for me! I am who I am. And it's not a defect! It's not a disability! And why did you pay? Why didn't you let me pay? What was that?" She opens her wallet and takes out bills. "How much?" She pushes three twenties across the counter toward Barbara. "I'm not an invalid!" What she means is, how could Barbara have said that after all this time they've spent together? Mylene, opening up to her. How could Barbara do this?

Barbara half closes her eyes and shakes her head. She's smiling. "Fucking little Mylie," she says. "Whiney Mylie. People don't change, do they?"

Mylene's face is hot.

"So I gave him the money. So what?"

"No, it's not like that. It's… Never mind."

"Walk away. Cry in a corner. So typical."

Mylene's throat has closed entirely. It's like Mary-Beth said—tension, stress, things that are uncontrollable. "In these situations," Mary-Beth told her, "it's the power of your will. And the breathing. Breathing, breathing, breathing." Mylene wants to tell Barbara that she's mean. Was mean and still is mean. She puts her hands on her knees, like she's been taught. She lets her belly fall, relaxes her shoulders, and inhales deeply into her rib cage, exhales through her mouth. Three times and then she stands, ready. "I'm happily married," she says even though she knows that she's twisting things. That this has nothing to do with Andy or their marriage. How stupid is she? How convoluted, how irrational? But it's Andy she's thinking of. She can't help it.

Barbara isn't looking at her. She's finished the beer and now she's flattening the cans one by one on the counter. A solid push with the heel of her hand, again and again. "It's bullshit," she says. "You are. Full of it. I've heard you. Your voice. You can scream all right. It's in there. Remember when you fell in that creek? When you almost drowned? Maybe you don't remember."

"I do," Mylene whispers.

"Oh my god. The noise! Me and Annie were petrified your mom would come charging down the hill. It was crazy what came out of you. If we hadn't been freaking out we would have been killing ourselves laughing. That frigging scream, I remember it. I mean. I'm telling you."

Mary-Beth Porczak said emotional and vocal extremes—singing or screaming—could release the voice. The analogy she used was hiccups. They can be stopped with a shock. It's the same but opposite is what she told Mylene.

"I know that," Mylene whispers. "That's the way it is with my condition." Mary-Beth didn't explain why Mylene can't perform at will. Why she has no control. "Give it time," she said. "The power is in you. You just have to find it. Unleash it."

"Like just now. You get mad and whoa! You should think about martial arts. You know? Get up your moxie, make some noise, do something. Honestly. You sounded fine shrieking about the money. Even though, who cares? I pay him, you pay him, who cares?"

Had her voice risen? Had she been loud and assertive? *Shrieking?* Mylene can't remember. Can't imagine. "You have a thing for him," she whispers. "Isaac. That's why you paid. I get it."

Barbara laughs then, a harsh sound. She looks at Mylene, her eyes wide, scarily white and wide, and says, "A: he's a Hutterite. And B: he's married. C: he has nine children. So no. I don't have a" —she makes air-quotes— "'thing' for him."

Mylene sits down. Tired. She is so tired. She wants her bed. She wants to be away from this place, away from Barbara. Why did she speak to her? What was she thinking? "Nine children?" she says. *"Nine?* What for?"

"Meaning, that's what. Purpose. It's their religion. They know about the meaning of life. Think about it."

Her car is working. She's free to leave. It's close to nine now. And she has to drive the highway. Two hours at least. She should get up. She should go home. It's dark. She thinks about livestock on the road. Deer. But she doesn't move.

"Why don't you like me?" she whispers.

Barbara looks right at her for a second in the way that only she can do, with frightening intensity, and a small smile that isn't really a smile at all. She shrugs. "Okay, yeah. I pushed you into the creek. I was mean to you. There you go. And why? I don't know. Because you were always hanging around? Because kids are shits? Because that's life? Because, just because? What are you gonna do about it? Maybe I thought you were contagious or something. If you came too close to me, kind of thing. Or I just wanted to push you. To smarten you up. And you survived, right? So no harm done. Your mom had a spaz attack, but she always had spaz attacks. That's the way she was. You can't go back and explain things. They happen. You move on. Whatever. And when you don't like someone, you don't like them. How can you explain it? And why should you?"

Mylene doesn't answer. There's nothing she can say. If you don't like someone, you don't. She sees herself as Barbara does—her neediness, her lack of strength. And here she is, still voiceless. "It's called spasmodic dysphonia, by the way. My condition. It's real."

"Your point?"

"That's what's wrong with me."

"Okay. Thanks for the info. Woo hoo."

"You stopped playing the piano. Your dream. So…"

Barbara stares straight ahead, immobile for a second, and then she rolls her eyes. "You wanna know what it's all about? What life is actually about? What's important?" The way her eyebrow twitches, the way her mouth quivers, slightly, as she pauses. She's going to reveal a secret truth, something that's been withheld from Mylene, who shrugs, wary, but also interested.

"Sex," Barbara says. Her tone is neutral and matter-of-fact, so that Mylene isn't sure if she's joking or serious.

But Barbara goes on. "It's all we focus on—movies, books, you name it. We read, watch, want—all we're thinking about, all the time, is sex. Creation. Make little people, that's what our bodies are driven to do. What we're told from the time we're born pretty much. And it's true. We want breasts. We want our periods. We want boys. We want to be pretty. We want to be sexy. For what? For breeding. Obviously. Call it what you want, but that's what we're here for. That's our purpose. Our destiny. Clothes, movies, pop songs—everything we're taught. You gotta get a guy, gotta get married, gotta have a kid. It's *biological*. It's everything. Because otherwise? If you don't have that? What are you gonna do? Paint? Write poetry? Make fucking clay pots? Grow petunias? Serve people apple pie and coffee? Play the piano? Yeah right. Anything to feel creative. We're made in God's image, right? That's what the Bible says. So like God—or whatever you want to call it—if we can't actually create, we have to create some way. To tell ourselves we're useful. Relevant. Ha. Piano. Singing. We're fooling ourselves. Bullshitting. Because we're useless. I am. You are. You get that, right? We have no value. Zippo. You and me both. We're kidding ourselves." She looks directly at Mylene then, and Mylene sees that the blue eyes are wet, that the blue make-up is running, that Barbie Kroondijk has been standing there, for she doesn't know how long, in the semi-darkness, crying.

"Isaac. That's what you're saying." Mylene feels the unnecessary truth in her words but she keeps going. "He's relevant and you wish you were. You wish you had what he has. Kids. A family. That kind of purpose." And then she thinks of the billboard, suddenly. JESUS IS THE ANSWER. Of course. This is what Barbara has been looking at for however many years. She almost laughs. And then she wants to reach out. She wants to touch Barbara, to hug her. But she doesn't, and for a second she's surprised at herself. That kindness is not as easy as it ought to be. "And now it's too late," she says, knowing as she speaks that she's saying the wrong thing.

"Music's a fraud. That's what I'm saying. It's bullshit."

Mylene gets up. Her hand is on her phone. Andy will be wondering why she isn't back yet, he'll be watching the ball game or the news, waiting for her. "I'm going to go now," she says.

"Sure. Gotta do what you gotta do. Me too, I guess. Got a pizza waiting for me. Still. Glad I could help. Old friends and all that." She fishes in her pocket and pulls out a pack of Juicy Fruit. Holds out a silver-foiled wrapped stick, which Mylene takes and puts in her purse because she doesn't chew gum, but she doesn't want to be rude.

"Thank you."

"No problem. It's been a slice. A stick. Stick, slice. Get it? Stick of gum. Slice of gum. Slice of life." She pours herself the rest of the wine, lights a cigarette, and sits down heavily, blowing smoke upward. "See you around."

Mylene hesitates for a second, shoulder against the door, and then she says, "But you're wrong, you know that? Because it is real. The piano or the singing or whatever it is. Serving coffee. Those things are real. And they're important." Her heart swells as she says this. It's a good feeling, but also unsettling, vaguely alarming. "Anyway," she says. "Thanks. I mean. Yeah. Thanks."

Barbara lifts her cigarette in a kind of wave, or dismissal. Her eyes are closed.

Outside it's completely still. No noise, no movement. The billboard looms dark and tall, and Mylene is reminded of the museum, the dinosaurs. She walks across the empty lot, careful not to stumble over asphalt pieces or metal debris. She tries to imagine the landscape as it used to be, the massive Albertosaurus galumphing across grassland, squealing or grunting or bellowing, but she can't. Because it's gone, she thinks. Ancient history. All that's left is a museum display. A tourist attraction you visit on your way to somewhere else.

DAIYU

RITA'S APPOINTMENT WITH THE SPECIALIST WAS THE DAY before Bruce's race. She's thinking about the diagnosis as she pulls out of their garage on her way to the finish line, where she'll wait and cheer with everyone else as the runners cross. Late afternoon light reflects the mess of her dashboard onto the windshield and for a few seconds the mirrored jumble divides her focus so she can hardly see. Loose pages, a hairbrush, garage opener, CDs, envelopes still sealed, pens, a stapler. It's the kind of mess that causes accidents, Bruce has told her. And she imagines it: the dull thud, the half-realization, and then oblivion. Her friend Evelyn told her about a woman who lay in a coma for nine months after a car crash. When she woke up her house had been sold and her husband introduced her to his new partner. Rita is never sure if this kind of story is told as a bleak comparison to her own situation, if it's thinly veiled advice, or if it's just a story. In any case, Evelyn, whom Rita has known her entire adult life, is a friend, and a distraction of sorts. Someone she can talk to. Someone who knows about Dani. Evelyn has told Rita that she and Bruce made a mistake. Some things, Evelyn says, aren't meant to be. They should have left well enough alone. Meaning Rita and Bruce should have remained childless; they should never have adopted Dani in the first place.

The specialist had been young, with fine hair and an open-necked shirt, his face round and boyish. He told her the newly formed growth in her abdomen was orb-like—a fluid-filled sac carrying liquid as clear as water adrift in her fallopian tube. She looked at him, watched the way his eyes stayed neutral, his smile noncommittal. He looked about one quarter her age. She'd expected something different. Glasses, a tie, grey hair. The kind of gravitas that came with age and the title "specialist." Also, she'd assumed he'd be a woman. He talked about rupture and complications and the fact that, despite this, surgery was elective—the growth could also disappear on its own. All this he said without making eye contact. "It's not something we can explain," he said. Of course, she was crying. Not because of the diagnosis, but also, yes, because of the diagnosis. She shook her head, said, okay, thank you, and left. It was that Dani had gone missing. The irony was too convoluted to explain.

Twenty minutes from the house she has to stop the car. A construction crew is replacing sewage pipes. It's been going on for the past three days. She should have considered it. Should have found an alternate route. Why hadn't she done that? This is the kind of logical thinking she's no longer capable of. So now she's stuck. She has no choice but to sit in the line of cars, inch when she's told to inch, stop when the car in front of her stops. The car clock reads 4:58. Based on the tracking app, Bruce will finish his race in forty minutes.

Since he's taken up the running, he's stopped reading the police reports, stopped sending international requests. He no longer checks the various websites. He ignores the endless tips. First it was marathons, but now he's into ultras. He set up the tracking app so she can follow him while he races. If she'd known about this kind of thing, she told him. He rolled his eyes and shook his head, indicating it was best not to go down that path. Hindsight. It's like a scourge. A drug to make herself feel better, and then worse. *If* she'd had a tracking app. *If* she'd called that day. *If* she'd put her foot down about the university on the other side of the country. *If* she'd monitored Dani's meds more diligently. *If* she'd found her a psychiatrist out there. *If.* The niggling self-destructive feeling that winding back the clock is an actual possibility.

If Bruce were having a real affair rather than this fling with himself. That also might make her feel better. The spotlight would be shining less squarely on her own inertia. Amplifying her sense of guilt a little less obviously. She can barely get out of bed in the morning. It's important to *feel*, Bruce says. And equally important not to wallow. "We have to get on with things," he says. "Our lives." And if it were a real affair she could be angry. They say anger is one of the stages. He's stopped eating sweets. "Brings me down," he says.

Traffic flows briefly from the other direction. The crane lifts a section of pipe and it swings heavily. She closes her eyes. Suicide is not uncommon in that age group, the officers said. "You have to be realistic." She didn't tell them she sees her in food courts, in the bank, on street corners; she's seen her in old women, in boys, in TV ads. The mind is a powerful thing.

And then she hears a shout and opens her eyes.

Ahead and to the right a man lifts a backpack and waves it in the air, yelling at drivers who refuse to look at him. She turns on the radio. The interviewer is earnest: "Can you tell us what that looked like?" She turns it off, opens the window to airless heat and the man's disjointed shouts. "Please... I need a ride... Come on... Motherfuckers!" She closes the window, turns on the air conditioner and feels the artificial breeze waft over her.

Bruce has gotten himself a coach. He's part of a running group. And then he came home with a treadmill for the den. The sound of him running is like that of an airplane taxiing for take-off. He creates his own artificial breezes. He suggested Dani's room for the contraption. "That way you won't be bothered by the noise."

When Dani was five, she hid under her bed and refused to come out.

The psychiatrist called it anxiety-disorder. Fear of change, he said, fear of death. These things were not unusual at that age. Minimize expectations, he said. Provide assurances. Years later, once they had the anxiety, which resurfaced in her teenage years, controlled with drugs and a psychiatrist's help, they joked about it with Dani: A nervous breakdown at age five! Rita dug up the phone recording she'd saved from Dani's first week in grade one when she'd called from the school office every day. "You'll be there to pick me up, Mummy? Promise you'll be there?" The tremulous pleading went on and on. To Rita and Bruce it had seemed an incomprehensible and unnecessary fear of nothing. And the nice thing about Dani was that she could listen to that old tape and laugh. "A writer, maybe?" Rita suggested. "All that emotion that's beyond your years and therefore frightening. You'll grow into it, I promise. Or maybe an actor and you can channel your worries. Put them into your characters." The world was a wonderful place, they told her. They were there for her, they said. The psychiatrist also suggested, at the very end of that first meeting—as though it was an afterthought, not actually important, not a fully formed idea, not a psychiatric theory—that perhaps something had happened to her? Something in her history? Were they aware of anything? If Rita could find him now, she'd ask what difference it would have made. If he would have told them to do anything otherwise.

Rita lies on Dani's bed after Bruce leaves for work and concentrates on forging a telepathic connection. Surely the room is still in Dani's head? Surely she's holding onto that, wherever she is. The exact shade of purple, the canopy bed, the whispering blinds. When Dani was nine she spent a weekend applying model paint to the glass of her geometrically shaped ceiling lamp. Tongue between her lips. The concentration unbreakable. The colours are separated by thick black lines.

Rita put her foot down. The treadmill would stay in the den. She'd get used to the noise.

When they first realized it was an impossibility for them, Bruce said it was okay. There was nothing special about having babies anyway. Anyone could do it, he said. And all they did was grow up. She'd been telling him about her childhood dolls. How she nurtured each one. She might have been crying. She still feels a deep sense of maternal longing, a bit like a swelling, when she thinks of those dolls—Polly, whose hair looked shiny green in certain light. Baby, who cried when she was squeezed and who arrived with a little glass bottle filled with milk-coloured liquid. She'd just assumed. She and Bruce were eating ice cream. He leaned forward and wiped a drip off her chin. Told her she was a sentimentalist and that they'd make it work.

The car in front of her is a Chevrolet. Vet. *Chèvre* (do French words count?). Vole (what does a vole look like?). Let. Love. Ever. Did they love her enough? Did they *ever* love her enough? Bruce says it's pointless to think that way. "You can't change the past." Thanks for that, Bruce. The steady noise of the fan is deafening. She turns it down and opens the window again. Hole. Hot. She shifts her legs on the leather. After his first race Bruce called from downtown. "Celebration! Come join us!" But Rita was already in bed. What time was it when he got in? Two? Three? Four in the morning? He climbed on top of her and pulled her cheeks wide. Pushed her face into the pillow with his forearm and panted in her ear. Feel this? he grunted. *This!* He thrust. *Is!* He thrust. *Life!* He thrust. *This!* He came. The next morning blood dripped from her anus into the toilet.

She adjusts her legs. Feels the leather. It's black and it burns when she gets in the car on a hot day. She's gained twenty-five pounds. She suffers headaches, spends days and nights in bed, mind and body thick with sleep. And then she endures long periods of insomnia when the idea of sleep looms as a mysterious impossibility. Her bedside table is lined with sleep aids. She tells Bruce she'll go back to the support group. But she won't. The last time she was there one of the women took her arm and said, "Do you find this helps? Even when there's no real hope?" The woman's son is in a halfway house six blocks from the church basement. "Bitch," Evelyn said. "What does she know?" Evelyn's son made the Varsity basketball team. "Can you believe it?" she shrieked. "It's a dream come true!"

Rita turns off the engine. There are at least ten cars behind her, another ten ahead. Or more. Someone somewhere behind her is honking. As if it will speed up the placement of the pipe.

"The most common thing," the officer told them, "is they call. Or they show up and say, oh sorry, were you looking for me? You know how it is. They're young. Self-centred. Responsibility's like a foreign word to them."

"Responsibility?" Bruce shouted. "*Responsibility?* You want to talk to me about *responsibility?* What are you cocksuckers doing? Hey? What are you actually, *physically,* doing?" He slammed his fist down.

The officer crossed his arms and waited. Then he said, "Finished? Because I get it. Believe me. We've seen it all."

The cramping—she pulls at the waistband of her skirt. Loosens it. It's like the orb needs room to breathe. Her orb. She strokes her belly. Imagines it. A *her.* A little she-orb that likes the touch, and is settling down. The specialist suggested losing weight would help alleviate the symptoms. She can feel the warmth of the swell under her hand. She'll put on Mozart for her when they get home.

Ahead of her, the flag lady's arms are bare and brown. The rest of her is encased in warning yellow. The CDs on the dash blink in the merciless sun, and she covers them with the pamphlets and papers she ought to clean up. The Pinyin lists, the music sheets, a report card. She took Mandarin lessons, she studied Chinese history, Chinese culture. She introduced Chinese New Year to Dani's school, had them celebrate the cherry blossoms, try moon cake and dumplings. They ate rice and noodles, they went for dim sum.

"There's no way you'll ever really understand her," Evelyn said. "No way. It's impossible, culturally and biologically."

"She's a kid," Rita said. "A little girl. The same needs and wants and fears and hopes as any girl. Give me a break." And they laughed. Because at that point, with their children on the swings or climbing the steps to go down the slide, problems being a cut knee or a broken wrist, they could laugh at anything. And hadn't Rita, over the years, been just as likely to call Evelyn out for mollycoddling her son? Evelyn was parent-liaison for every one of his sport teams, PTA president his entire high school career. "He's sick of you," Rita said. "Give him his space, why don't you? You'd be surprised." The words you want to take back. There could be a sister somewhere is what she thinks about now. Dani could be with her sister. Comparing facial features. Personality traits.

The specialist said he'd prefer to eradicate. That's the word he used. It was the safer option, he said.

The Chevrolet moves and the man with the backpack appears again. Walking beside the traffic. He's in dirty runners, no socks, dirty jeans that are too short in the leg. He shouts at the flag lady, his backpack beating punctuation, and she shouts back. Rita can't distinguish the words, but the animosity shimmering between them is palpable. His anguish versus her professional determination, both equally convinced they're right. She wants to lean in and catch the nuances. Feel what they feel. Absorb their certainty.

She should get a job, Evelyn says. To shift her focus. "There's nothing you can do, you have to get that through your head. That's life." Sometimes Rita looks through the listings—clerical work, retail, teacher's aide—and wonders how she would explain her requirement for mental health days. Some days, walking through doors is impossible. Every small, sober-faced, black-haired female wearing a leather bomber is Dani.

Even though she could be anything anywhere by now. She could be wearing a sari in India; she could be in handcuffs in Mexico; she could be on a beach, or in a ditch. She could be dead. Or she could be in China. "After a certain period..." the officers said. "Sometimes a ceremony is the thing. Closure. You know. So you can move on."

The flag lady lowers the stop sign and cars start to move slowly, Rita with them. A slight breeze, a feeling of forward momentum, but then, when she's right beside the woman, the sign goes back up. She tries to smile, to show that she understands the rules, the need for cooperation. But she can't. Because it feels personal. That raised sign.

"Is what it is," the woman says. She has a sunburn. She's covered it with make-up, which makes her skin heavier, paler and almost plastic, but her ears and her neck are red. Her forehead is peeling. She holds the sign and stares over the line of cars, avoiding their questions and impatience. Rita recognizes the coping strategy.

In grade nine Dani's Social's class studied China. One-child policy, human rights atrocities, poverty, communism versus capitalism, history, the cultural revolution, Tiananmen Square. The teacher asked if this would be all right for Dani. Would it upset her? As though Dani hadn't lived her entire life in Canada. The question of Dani's loyalties, her affiliation. Her nature. That these could be questions.

On the other side of the car the man with the backpack shouts again. "Fucking bitch! All I want..." His face is flushed. He's sweating. Rita can feel his heat creep over her, settle right into her bones. His pain. Yes, she thinks: *All I want...!* The delay is too much. Unreasonable. Unbearable. In that moment she wants the man to hit the flag lady, who has planted her feet wide and let the sign drop to direct her full attention toward the man.

"You want me to call my supervisor?" she shouts. "Is that what you're after? Hey? That I get the cops involved? I told you. You can't walk here! It's dangerous."

Rita inches forward. Because the sign is down. Because of the man. The woman's voice. Her stance. Her combativeness. Her confidence.

"Hey!" The flag lady thrusts the sign in front of Rita's windshield.

And suddenly the view is not big enough. The sun, the machinery, the shouting, the honking, the flag lady and her strident commands. The car is too small, too constricted, too painful. She can't sit here. She can't breathe. She's being smothered. Her life is too small. Too much. Dani and Bruce and the support group. Evelyn with her smug self-satisfaction. The flag lady with her plastic make-up armour and her yellow caution suit. The heat. The line-up. The endless, endless waiting.

She sweeps her arm across the dash. One wide, hard movement. Pushes everything—lists, envelopes, hair clips, phone charger, stapler, CDs, dust—everything—onto the passenger seat, the floor, the console.

She gets out of the car, pointing and asking, "What gives you the right?"

"Excuse me?"

"Just because you—"

"Get back in your car."

"Why *can't* he walk here? Why can't he? Just because you're holding a sign?" She's shaking her head, waving an arm to indicate the workers, the traffic, the man. The heat in her face and head. "Is that why? Because you can? Is that it?" But then her voice falters.

"Ma'am."

She's breathing hard.

"Ma'am!"

The man is watching her and she's aware of the flag lady speaking into her radio, using words like "situation" and "warning." She hears the honker honking, someone whistling. People are leaning out of their car windows. Or they've opened their doors and are standing beside their cars, watching.

"You don't understand." She's trying to continue. She wants to. She wants to be angry. To have a reaction. A reason. Evelyn's voice is right there. *I told you so.* She can't get away from it. Evelyn's son will play basketball or he'll quit and she'll shift gears and focus on his next feat. The inevitability—that's what she feels. That life goes the way it will. With you or without you. Her baby, her Dani-girl—wet head wrapped in the pink towel with ears, the black eyes, fingers plinking the Fisher-Price piano keys, banging on the drum set. Squatting in front of cartoons. Ballet slippers. The streamers on her bike. Skipping ropes. Slurping noodles. She wore a Robin Hood costume her first Halloween. The dress-up box is still in the garage. The neighbour kids. Oh, Dani. Daiyu. They thought her name would make things difficult. Her beautiful name. Daiyu, which means black jade and promises strength. Daiyu. That was what they'd worried about. Her name.

Hand on her orb, Rita looks right at the flag lady. "This could be—" she says, her hand making circles. "I could be… I could be…" Nodding. Like there's some kind of certainty. Some kind of truth. "You have no idea. About me. About him. About anything." She moves to the other side of the car, and just like that, eyes on the flag lady, she opens the passenger door and indicates to the man that he should get in. Which he does. He climbs into the car as though it's the natural thing to do. He sits on top of the papers and the CDs and holds tight on his knees the backpack, which is pink and filthy.

The flag lady is looking at her in disbelief, raising a hand, opening her mouth, shaking her head, but Rita is already in the driver's seat. She's already closing the window. She takes hold of the wheel and concentrates on the Chevrolet.

Lover. Her torso under Bruce's weight. She'd focussed on small, quick breaths. He'd rolled off her, heavy and exhausted. Eyes closed, he went on and on, saying he loved her, he needed her, his voice watery, weepy. And she said nothing, did nothing, felt nothing. He comes in from his runs, exhilarated, stripping off his wet singlet to expose his sweating midriff, self-assured in a way Rita can't fathom. "Running is all about control," he says. "Taking charge." Once, he pushed her face into the fridge, hitched up her skirt and took her hard. Once it was in the garage. The bruises on her arms shone yellow before they faded.

She puts her hand on the gearshift. Lever. She's forty-nine years old. Volt. She has a growth in her belly. This is something she knows. Something she can feel. It belongs to her, this growth. Surgery is the logical route. The specialist smiled as he said this, as though the words would be reassuring. "My daughter was a cutter," she told him. But she didn't say it out loud. She'd left Band-Aids and Polysporin in Dani's room, pamphlets for teen counselling services. *Are you feeling overwhelmed?* in gentle green sloping letters. Bruce says it was genetics. "There are things we'll never know. Predispositions. The like." They would look after her is what they'd promised, not once, but over and over again. A better home than what she would have had, that's what they promised. Protection.

Revolt.

She starts the car, and, as though from another world, the clock blinks. It takes a few seconds before she remembers the app—the running. Bruce. She should have been there by now. She should be watching, cheering him through the last stretch. His first ultra-marathon competition. The sweat-bathed shirt, the strain, the fatigue on his face when he lifts his arms and crosses the finish line. The satisfaction. She won't be there to witness that. According to the app's estimate he'll be finished when she gets there. She was already cutting it close, even without the roadwork delays. And now there's no way she'll get there in time.

Cheer.

When she gets home she'll look it up. Maybe there's an app for this game too. How many words can you make out of Chevrolet?

Echo. Heel. But not heal.

She pulls the seat belt across her chest. Heat shivers above the hood of the car. She could take him home with her, this man in the passenger seat beside her. He's rocking forward and back, the backpack on his knees. His smell fills the entire car. He has a scar above his eye and his face is pockmarked. She could set the dining room table. Get out the crystal glasses, the silver, her grandmother's dishes. He'd be there when Bruce got home. "There's a man in the bathroom," she'd say. "He's in the tub." She keeps her eye on the stop sign, waiting for it to be lowered, and wonders what little girl has lost or given away or just forgotten about the pink backpack that once upon a time would have been shiny new and exactly what she wanted.

LOT

LOT'S FEET HAVE GROWN HEAVY. HER ANKLES ARE swollen and her body aches with the sitting. She's in the back seat of her son's Volvo watching the scenery run on and on, huge open spaces on one side of the endless highway and a forest of black trees on the other. The size, the rawness of the land, the emptiness. Indecent, she thinks. An assault to her eyes, this naked sprawl. But she doesn't say it out loud. She is here, in Canada, to visit Bram, whom she hasn't seen for six years. And to meet Jodi, his partner, who has short dark hair and teeth that are unnaturally white, and who twists in her seat to ask again if Lot is comfortable, if she wouldn't rather have the front.

No, Lot says. She is fine, yes.

Beside Lot, Jodi's dollhouse takes up half the back seat. Three storeys of miniature perfection, the toy house is the exact replica of a Victorian mansion—wainscoting and papered walls, tiny carpets, moulding, railings, bathroom fixtures. The furniture, Jodi explained, is in the trunk, packed safely in sheets of tissue so it doesn't get damaged on the drive. Jodi and Bram have shared a home for five years, and so far there has been no talk of marriage or children or a *real* life together. Jodi is a teacher and Bram is an accountant. He has always had a head for numbers. In this way he is the same as his father was—no room for the everyday practical. Forty years of marriage, forty years in the same house, sitting at the same kitchen table, and still the man had no idea where Lot kept the coffee and the tea.

"You see how the forest has changed, Lot? See how it keeps getting worse and worse as we go north and west?"

Lot. Even the neighbour, whom she's known more than thirty years, calls her *Mevrouw.* And the forest is dead. As though the nuclear threat had been real. Over the past few days the trees have gone from green to red and red-brown to black. Of course she sees it. What else is there to see? At home the forest is fresh and organized and there is no problem. "Why they do not stop this beetle?"

"I know." Bram shakes his head.

Lot notices the grey over his ears. The fine lines around his eyes. Six years since he's visited her in Holland. He had to travel to Rotterdam and Brussels for meetings. He came home for lunch and said he was fortunate to have time to see her at all. The neighbour snorted and said he was probably going to the "cafés" in Amsterdam. She was not impressed by the casual clothing, which Lot now sees is typical. Jodi has worn nothing but shorts and sleeveless shirts. Bram is the same. Legs and arms draped everywhere.

"It's horrible," Bram says.

We are of the same ilk, Lot thinks. The delicate complexion. The sensitivity. When he was three and four he used to promise he would always be her boy.

Jodi shakes her head, shrugs one bare shoulder. "Oh, come on. It's nature's way. We can wring our hands and whine about plague and drought and global warming, but that's just the way it goes. You adjust. This'll make room for new species, new trees, whatever. It's like a forest fire. Totally natural."

"Most forest fires are started by morons, not nature," Bram says. "It's humans causing the problems, Jo. You gotta admit it."

"Humans are natural, Bub." She leans over and kisses him on the cheek, the neck, the shoulder. His puts his hand on her thigh.

Lot smooths her skirt, turns her head to look at the black trees. They've been driving for three days, sleeping in campgrounds where people play loud music and have roaring fires. Bram and Jodi raise the tents, and then Jodi opens the cooler and roots around, pulling out beers, cucumbers and tomatoes, soggy cheese and hamburger patties. There has not been a proper place to walk, or sit with a coffee and a *gebakje*. It is like the wilderness has gripped the people and stopped them remembering that they are civilized.

"Chil-co-tin. What does this mean?" she asked when she saw the sign.

"'People of the red ochre river,'" Jodi said. "I wikkied it. Red. Ochre. River. Don't you love it?" As though the stress on each word made the meaning more significant.

They are headed north and west to the Pacific Ocean, where a ferry will take them through what Bram describes as fjords that rival Norway's, to the island where they will visit a dollhouse show that begins the day after tomorrow. "People from all over Canada and the U.S. will be there," Jodi said. "It's a perfect opportunity to kill two birds with one stone." This expression she explained slowly and carefully. As though Lot were a schoolchild. Lot has been to Norway. In 1961 she and her husband went to see an art exhibition in Oslo. She has seen the fjords.

"Oh, wait! Check that out." Jodi sits up and points ahead. Lot prepares to hear about another rock with a name, or a dry gulch, or a creek. But no. Jodi is pointing to a vehicle that is stopped at the side of the road. Its hood is up and Lot shifts to better see the truck and beside it the man who is waving to get their attention, both arms in the air. Lot's cardigan and blouse and undergarments stifle her. She is hot, but more than that, she needs to go to the toilet. The flight and all this driving— her abdomen is hard and full. Painful. The endless sitting. Her back, her legs. When she moves, her insides emit a noise, and Jodi turns. "Are you all right?"

One *keutel* in the concrete bunker that housed the facilities at the last campsite. A rabbit dropping, no more. "I am fine. Yes."

Bram swerves across the highway and slows to a stop so that the front of the car is almost touching the front of the truck, which is old and green and rusted, a sort one does not see at home. Lot grips the back of Jodi's seat. *"Niet stoppen!"* she hisses. "You know not this person. What will you do?" For surely this is dangerous! But Bram does not heed her—he gets out of the Volvo, so that Lot takes a sharp breath. Bram has never shied from danger. As a child he was a bolter, running straight at everything.

"Hello!" Bram is almost shouting. As though this stranger is an old friend.

The man is thin and wears a ball cap, jeans, and a shirt that is half-open. Lot cannot see his face, cannot understand what is being said. Hot breeze floats through the open windows of the car. Crickets or birds, voices. The words are lost to her.

"Well," Jodi says. "I mean…"

"What?" Lot asks. "Is there not any help? A towing truck? What will Bram do for this man? He is not… My son. He is not…" She looks at her lap, but she cannot find the words. Bram has clean fingernails, clean hands. Surely Jodi knows this.

"He's pretty handy, Lot."

"He is *not* a handy."

"Anyways." Jodi shrugs. "He might as well try, right?" And then she reaches into the back and Lot flinches. She pushes her hands into the pockets of her cardigan and worries her handkerchief. But Jodi does not touch her. She wants only to rearrange the dollhouse, which slid forward when Bram stopped. Lot knows that Jodi is waiting for her to say something, to comment on the workmanship, the precision. She has been waiting for this since the beginning of the trip. But Lot has said nothing. She cannot believe a grown woman spends her time like this.

"The furniture is perfect," Jodi says. "Wait till you see it all put together. Every piece an exact copy. Including the dishes. I even have a sewing machine." She smiles at the house as though it were alive, a child, an infant that needs her attention. "I think I told you it took me two years? It's slow work. I had to use a magnifying glass for most of it. And my fingers!" She holds them out, but Lot sees nothing out of the ordinary. Short, blunt fingers. The girl will never be a piano player. "It's the continuity. You know? Being able to work on something until it's perfect? It's not like that at school. The kids?" She shakes her head. "Before you know it, it's June and you feel like there's still so much to do."

Lot lifts her chin in the direction of the truck because Jodi needs to change her focus. To watch what is going on. Does she not recognize the danger?

"There's nothing out here, Lot," Jodi says, turning to look. "I mean. Think about it—there's no gas station, no tow truck. That's just the reality in these parts. You gotta help each other."

Jodi speaks as though Lot might not be seeing what is obvious. She speaks as though what Bram is doing is perfectly all right, with no acknowledgement of the kinds of things that might happen. Bram tells Lot he is happy, says *they* are happy. Of course, he is a grown man. He has been in this country nineteen years. She supposes it is a fine thing that he has met someone. Her neighbour has six grandchildren. They clamber on her furniture and wade through the flower beds after their *voetbal*, leaving the neighbour with nothing but cleaning to do when they go home. She changes diapers and has to bottle-feed the babies. She bakes for them. Tells Lot *boterkoek* is their favourite. As if she is the only woman who can bake *boterkoek*. As if grandchildren are the only reason one does things.

"Jo!" Bram shouts. "Can you pop the hood?"

Jodi stretches across the driver's seat, reaching for the release so that Lot sees the length of her arm muscles, the curve of her breast. The straps of Lot's brassiere dig into her shoulders. Her legs stick to the upholstery. Right through her stockings.

"All right, now rev it, babe!" With the hood up they can no longer see him.

Jodi moves over. She is fluid and quick, turning the key, pressing the gas pedal without hesitation so that the engine is loud immediately. "Okay?" she shouts out the window. "Is that enough? Do you want me to do it again?"

Heat weighs down the car. Lot puts her head back and closes her eyes. They had told her the trip would be long. Over tea with her neighbour, Lot held out the map, the ticket, the plans, explained that she wanted to do this. That she wanted to see how he lives. And here she is. This is what life is like in Canada. There is work and space. It is a perfect place, Bram says. The neighbour has never been in a tent. Never been away from home.

"There will be a bed this night? On this boat?" Lot asks. They will be on the ferry, Jodi has told her. It will be an adventure, she said, a story to take home.

Jodi looks at her through the rear-view mirror. "Wait. You're not all right, are you? I knew it. I mean. I told Bram it might be too much. I told him. The bathroom? Is that it? Because we could stop somewhere. You know." Yesterday Jodi squatted behind a bush and Lot heard her void. She came back laughing, saying she had to use grass to wipe. Bram rolled his eyes and told her there was tissue in the car. And then he took hold of her hands and kissed her lips.

The hood slams shut.

"Nothing." Bram's voice carries on the hot air. In two months he is going to be a Canadian citizen. Lot sucks in her cheeks. Not even dual. "Never going back." He laughed when she asked. In the row house, she hasn't changed his room. The same narrow bed against the wall, sheets and blankets pulled tight and smooth, blue and white striped curtains open during the day and closed at night. He used to love the American football. Pennants and posters and caps. All of these are still in his room. And his books. His memories. The neighbour tells her she is foolish to hang onto these things. "If he wants them, let him come and get them," she says. "It could be your sewing room. Or you could rent it out." The neighbour does not understand.

Jodi opens the door wide. "Bram? We're not trying again?" But Bram is talking to the man, his back to the Volvo.

"I guess that didn't work," Jodi says to Lot. "Anyways, it's all about the experience, isn't it? That's Bram for you. Always wanting that elusive authentic. He loves it. He's the one who got all excited about showing you this. I mean, me too, of course. Don't get me wrong. But he's all about going for it. The genuine thing. That's what he's after. You know?"

They watch Bram gesture toward the highway, tip his head to the side. The way his shoulder lifts, the quiver in his hand, the way his legs are poised to move all remind Lot of her little son, little Brammetje, his blue eyes innocent and trusting. His hand in hers, pulling for her to hurry up. The number of times she had to dash after him. Catch him before he ran onto the street. Even then she had the beginnings of arthritis in her hip. Bunions on both feet. She was forty-one when she had him. She considered him a miracle. Her husband had told her to give up hope.

"Don't you think? That's what he's like, right?" Jodi looks at Lot expectantly.

Lot says nothing. What does Jodi think? That they are going to sit here in the hot Volvo, Lot squeezed against the empty dollhouse, in the middle of nowhere, and talk together about *her* son?

"Whoa. Can you smell that?" Jodi sniffs the air. "Is it a fire? It's a fire, right? Do you see the smoke? It's pretty close by, I'd say." And then she calls outside, "Bram?"

"He was not always a good boy." Lot rubs one thumb over the other.

Bram says something to Jodi, who nods and settles back into the seat. "It's far away. Someone burning garbage, apparently. That's what he says. Not to worry." Then she turns, as though she has only now heard Lot's words. "A good boy? You mean Bram?" She laughs. "What kid is? I mean, I stole money from my mom's purse and I used to lie all the time. Really, who doesn't? That's just kids. That's what kids do. Seriously, I see it all the time. Wouldn't it be the same in your day? Or did you…? Was it different? I mean, I guess I don't know what it's like there, and, back then, what with the war, right? That's got to affect a nation, obviously. Oh my god, the smell." She puts her hand over her nose and mouth. "It's toxic for sure. Guaranteed."

Lot tries to arch her back to relieve pressure. "We sit," she says. "This is what we do. You. You do not help."

"Oh god! Jeez. I'm sorry. Maybe we should get out for a bit, okay? While we wait? It'd be good, right? Stretch a little? It's a long drive, I know." She swings her legs out of the car and stands as she speaks. Everything about her is quick. Too quick, too definite. "It's…" Jodi's hand hovers in front of her pelvis. "Blocked up, right? Like, with the time change and all? And the sitting? Wreaks havoc with the plumbing, I know. I feel for you, really, I do." Her wide eyes, her confidence—it is abrasive, and Lot does not respond. She climbs out of the Volvo, slowly, carefully. Her back is a knot, her hip aches, and her intestines tighten as she moves. Jodi holds her elbow and together they take a few steps away from the car. "Worse or better?"

Lot takes another tentative step. Of course it is not better. Any fool can see this. On the first day, in the city, she walked easily. They walked around the block, bought the newspaper. When they stopped in the mountains the next day, she walked to the lake and looked at the water, which was brown and dull and grassy, not at all as Canadian water should be. She was disappointed and waited at the picnic table while Bram and

Jodi hiked. Bram told her she'd missed seeing a deer. She told him she did not feel well, that she preferred to sit. Did he not remember that there are deer at home?

"Jodi? Ma?" Bram has his hand on the back of the thin man. "This is Victor," he says. "He's gonna come with us."

And then Lot sees. The man Bram has been talking to is an Indian. She looks from her son to the man, whose eyes are black and whose cheeks are old leather. Ready to crack. Like a shoe she would throw away.

"Nice to meet you." Jodi stretches out her hand, but the man does not take it. He lifts his chin by way of greeting and then he turns to close the hood of the dirty truck. He wipes his hands on his jeans and makes a noise in his throat so that Lot steps back. She pulls her cardigan tight.

Bram turns to Jodi, eyebrows raised. "We don't really have a choice." His eyes are a question, and then he says something else and Jodi's head and shoulders move. So much of what they say Lot cannot follow. Abbreviated English that hides meaning. And the silent signals are worse. A lifted finger, the twitch of a lip, the slight narrowing of eyes.

"Honestly, it's not a problem," Jodi says to Bram, and then she looks at the man. "Don't worry about it, Victor. You sit in the front. We'll squeeze into the back. There's tons of room. Right, Lot?"

They want to take this man with them in the Volvo. This stranger.

"Ma?"

Lot does not move. It is beyond her understanding. All of what they do. What will be next? She cannot bear it. She wants to lie on her back and close her eyes. She wants to lie on her back in her own bed with her pillow under her knees, the curtains drawn. She wants a cup of tea. Her tea. In her cup.

"Are you wanting to get in first? Is that it? Or do you want the door? And then I can sit by the dollhouse? Would that be better?"

And then Lot cannot respond to Jodi's endless questions. Her breath is caught. Caught in her throat because now she sees that behind the cracked windshield of the broken truck there are more of them. The truck is full of Indians. Can this be? The sun is too bright. Lot squints, and yes, yes! She sees their dark hair behind the glass. Children clambering up and down over the seats, the dashboard, over an old woman who has a face like a dried apple and who stares straight ahead.

Lot clutches her son's arm and points. "*Kijk!*" Because perhaps her son has not seen them.

"I know. But what are we going to do? Victor's gonna come back. With his cousin. To pick them up. Don't worry about it."

There are three children, Lot sees. And the woman. The woman!

"They'll be totally fine," Jodi says. "And Victor's gonna be right back with help."

"You know not," Lot says to her. "You." She plants her feet wider on the pavement. "No. We do not do this. I do not." The heat, the stink of fire, the hardness of her belly. The choices her son makes so carelessly, so thoughtlessly. For it is one thing to take the man. But it is another to leave the family. She will not be part of this. She will not.

"What else are we going to do?" Jodi's voice rises. "Come on. Please, Lot. Think about it. The ferry, right? We have to make it. I have the dollhouse show. Remember? Remember why we're here?"

"Dollhouse!" Lot pulls her chin in tight, nostrils flaring. "Dollhouse!" She puts one hand on the Volvo roof and with the other she opens the back door. The sunlight gleams on the shingles of the perfect replica and Lot has to blink against it. She raps the painted wood with her knuckles. "What is this?" she asks. "Do you see? This. What do you do? It is not for playing. It is not... It is not... It has not any...*punt*." There is no fluidity, the words come out wrong and she is not sure they understand what she is trying to say. But she continues. "Why we do not leave this house? Here. By the road. I... I will not..." And then the words burst through. "*Je kan kiezen. Of ik, of het poppenhuis!*" She folds her arms over her chest and stands as tall as she is able, firm in her ultimatum. Her, or the house. "You," she says to Jodi. "You have not any children." She holds her mouth in a tight line. It is a stupid language, this English.

"What?" Jodi throws up her hands. "What are you saying? Okay, Bram. This is..."

"Get in the car, Ma. That's enough."

But Lot does not get into the car. She turns away from Bram. Away from Jodi and the Volvo, the truck and the Indians. She starts to walk, placing one foot deliberately and carefully in front of the other, feeling her weight transfer from side to side. Every step solid.

"What are we supposed to do?" Jodi cries out. "Like, what the hell does she expect? She thinks I'm gonna leave my dollhouse? Because we have no kids? Is that what she's saying? Oh my god. Oh my god! And now what? What are we going to do? We have a schedule!"

"You think there's no room for you, Ma? Is that what you think? We're trying to help these people! That's what we're doing, for Christ's sake."

Lot keeps walking, one foot in front of the other, steady.

"Oh my god! This is... And what? Now we have to come back for her? I can't believe her! This is... She's insane!"

"Fuck it. We don't have time for this. We're going. We're going."

She hears his voice clearly, as though he were right beside her. She hears the car doors close, the engine; she hears the car move away and pick up speed. And she is not surprised. Not surprised at all. Bram did not come back for the funeral of his father. Too expensive, he said. Not a good time. Lot did not argue. She did not say that he would be coming for her sake. That his father was already dead.

The dry, hot air makes the inside of her nose hurt. She feels the swell of her abdomen. The pain in her feet. And then the fear, rising. But she pushes onward, concentrating on the edge of the road in front of her, on the grass clumps that have forced their way through the asphalt, on the white line that appears and fades and reappears. She will not think of them. The heat, the distance, the futility, what does it matter? They will come back. Of course they will. She curls and uncurls her fingers, and it is not so bad. It is better. She can feel her blood moving, her hip loosening. Twenty steps, thirty steps. The pavement is unforgiving under her feet. They will come back and because of this perhaps they will miss the ferry. Her shoulders and neck, her hips—the movement is good. Forty steps, fifty. They will have to look for her, she'll walk that far.

"Lady!" A shrill, small voice, so that at first Lot thinks it is a bird. A raven with a voice like a child's. These too, they have at home. Jodi did not believe her. You must mean a crow, she said to Lot, but no, Lot did not mean a crow. She meant a raven. Jodi. So certain about everything.

"Laaay-dee!"

Lot turns to see a small girl skipping and running down the shoulder of the road. Loose arms and bare feet, she appears weightless, floating. The girl runs until she is in front of Lot, and then she stops and pushes flyaway strands of hair, more dust-coloured than black, out of her eyes. She looks up at Lot and says, "You're not s'pose to walk." She is breathing easily, relaxed despite the running, and there is no expression on her face, no sweat or sign that she is affected by the heat. "You hafta get in the truck, that's why. Her said."

Lot does not know how to respond, what to do. Now that she has stopped moving, her head prickles from the heat, and blood pulses in her hands, which are thick and too heavy. The girl is from the truck, of course. An Indian child sent to get her.

"Her's my grandma."

Lot places her pulsing hands on her abdomen and looks past the girl to where the truck rests, idle and broken. The Indian woman has sent the child and now Lot is supposed to go and sit in that truck. She snorts. It is the nerve of this country, of these people, Jodi, Bram, all of them. This child, who shows no fear, no *respect*. Her skin is grey-brown, and there are pale spots on the tops of her feet and on her shins. Water, Lot realizes. Drops of water have fallen onto her skin and dried there.

It would be nice, some water. She takes out her handkerchief. Touches it to her forehead, upper lip, her throat.

The girl does not stop moving. She lifts her arms and spins in a circle, round and round, hair and body following thin outstretched arms. Half-naked in her soiled, sleeveless dress that is threadbare and hangs low in front, she steps lightly, barefoot on the pavement, as though all of this—the broken truck, the heat, the stink—is nothing.

Burdened, this is how the child makes Lot feel. Unwieldy. The sturdy black shoes so cumbersome, and her stockings, so unnecessary. The idea of walking down this never-ending road. She could travel the entire day and arrive nowhere. There is no end to it. She could die here and it would go unnoticed. Her eyes begin to water. She blinks and presses her handkerchief to the bridge of her nose. "It is the stink," she says. "It is a very bad stink."

"Jesse gots a fire and now it's gonna go everywhere," the girl says. "That's why her said you hafta."

Lot looks at her again, and then she wants to touch her, suddenly. To take the little hands into her own and hold them close. It is almost unbearable, this longing. She smiles at the girl, reaches out to her. It has been nineteen years since Bram left home, and her husband has been dead eight. Still she is not used to it. The loneliness. "Come," Lot says. "Come here." But the child doesn't pause. She continues to skip back and forth, oblivious.

And then Lot wants to say that her dress is dirty, that her skipping is not smooth, that she should be afraid of something. She wants to say it loudly and harshly.

But she does not. She is not of this child's world. Her words mean nothing here. She feels the burning of her eyes, the thickening of her throat. The ache. She closes her eyes against it, and then she sinks.

Her joints fail—her hand is out, her body knows what's coming, but she cannot stop the fall.

The child sees, and she comes to stand over Lot, staring down at her, and Lot waits. But the child says nothing. She does not offer to help—it is as though she cannot understand, as though she does not recognize what is needed. Or does not want to. The dark eyes are impenetrable.

And so Lot stays on the ground. She looks into the distance where, far beyond the yellow fields, beyond the hills and the mountains, the horizon cuts a distinct line, the end of the blue-green land and the beginning of the blue-blue sky clearly defined. At home it is not like this. At home the sky and the earth blend together, the division blurred and gentle. Here it is hard. Even the sun, even the earth, bald and harsh. Hard. That her son has chosen this place to live. With Jodi and her dollhouse. Dollhouse. This toy of hers, which will never see happiness—children running through its rooms, a family breathing life into its perfect walls. Lot cannot help it—she thinks again of the room upstairs in the row house. She is a fool. This is what she is. A fool.

The girl speaks out of nowhere. "That's why stuff grows more stronger. Because the fire. And that's why we hafta have smoke."

The ease of her movements. The loose limbs and bare feet. Lot sees all this as though for the first time.

"*Ja*," she says. "*Zo is het*." She will not weep. She will not.

She looks at the child a moment longer and then she leans forward and begins to undo the laces of her shoes. She will free her feet. Because it's as the neighbour says, *praktisch*. She will remove her stockings and feel the breeze on her skin. And it will be fine. It will be better.

EXIT STRATEGY

HE TELLS ME TO GO HAVE A LOOK IN THE BARN. "USED TO keep them horses in there," he says. "Near and Far. That's what I called them." He glances at me, eyes narrowed. "Near and Far," he says again. Weighing my reaction, I suppose. There's a canniness about him, I noticed it right away, this need to gauge, assess and reassess. He's sharp, or at least, he's used to being sharp. His name is Mick. He's eighty-six years old and he sits in a semi-broken wheelchair whiling away time between doctor's appointments. A grey cat is draped over the blanket on his lap. Perhaps I should feel sorry for him, old and ill as he is, but my inclination tends toward the practical, empathy being one of the subtle emotions that have eluded me since the accident. That along with compassion and the ability to properly love. So I'm told by my daughter Hazel. She says it's as though I'm on a platform, looking down at human activity like a child might look at Lego pieces. Where others see individuals and their hardships, I see the shuffling of inanimate blocks, the setting up and taking down of obstacles, the attaching and detaching of tiny parts. That's what she tells me. "You're hard," she says. "Cold." It may be true that I sometimes appear removed from the world, but maybe I've always been that way.

The accident was two years ago in a small country in Asia where driving skills are centred on the ability to exert repeated and rapid pressure on the horn. I was in the back seat.

The result was eight months of hospital beds and rehabilitation and although my bones knitted tidily—pelvis, clavicles, humerus (both arms), mandible—some aspects of my mind have remained tangled due to head injuries sustained. I used to be an actuary but now I suffer headaches that stultify. They strike at inopportune times, numbing my brain. This means my immediate financial subsistence revolves around insurance cheques rather than paycheques. Which is one of the reasons I'm here: a cash job, under-the-table. My savings were put to work well before the accident. Hazel needed help with her student loans; Hazel needed a down payment. Now, when I'm laid low, my reasoning powers—my ability to categorize logically, rationally, to think like a normal adult—go out the window. Hazel questions my ability to look after Chance, my three-year-old grandson. That's the other reason I'm here. She's forbidden me access. And so I look at the photos she sends— Chance eating cookie dough, Chance in the dog basket, the dog licking Chance's face. On a bad day I can't figure out if the dog's eyes or the boy's eyes are related to me. It might get worse, Hazel says.

What I see in Mick's barn is a weathered sailboat. It has a wooden cabin, a wooden hull, wood planking, and it rests on a series of sawhorse-like structures that have been jimmied and joined to form makeshift scaffolding. Stepladders are positioned starboard and portside as points of entry. I've been on the property a day-and-a-half. I'm here for an undetermined length of time to help Mick with farm chores, housecleaning, cooking, and personal hygiene as necessary. I have no medical training and no experience with husbandry, but in the phone interview he told me that would be fine. He could still see, still talk. He still knew how things had to be done. "Mind's sharp as a tack," he said. Tumours accumulate in his body even as he endures treatment. His eyes are rheumy-blue, cheeks and lips pale and drawn. He has no hair under his ball cap. He's small. I imagine him shrinking, his spine crumbling in front of me.

He looked me up and down when I arrived. I'd been on the long-haul bus for six hours and then a short-haul the remaining three, my eyes and whole body tight against fear that clenched my insides. He said I'd do, and then in the next breath he told me the wind would blow me over, I was that skinny. "No way you're gonna be capable of what I need." A leaping mind—that much we have in common.

He plans to fix the boat, he tells me, then climb aboard with Coombs the owl that has a broken wing and lives in a ten-foot-square cage in one of the outbuildings. Together they'll float the 100-kilometre length of the lake. Last night a hollow whooo-whooo made me appreciate deeply and almost weepily the freedom of country living and then this morning he showed me the cage and introduced me to the Great Horned Owl that had flown into his truck grill. The vet told Mick the bird would be dead by morning, but Coombs has been in the cage eight years, waiting stoically for the dead rodents Mick brings him every few days, snared in traps that line the barn walls, the edges of the kitchen and mudroom. There was an eviscerated rabbit on the floor of the cage when Coombs and I were introduced. The whole property reeks of decline. Entire boards are missing from the hull of the boat and the gaping holes expose a skeletal frame. The windows are broken and there's no motor, no sign of mast or boom or sails. He tells me Coombs is getting pissed off. "That's the way it is. I can't always get around. Some days I can't get myself outta this goddamned chair." He asks if I know how to bait traps. If I'm okay handling dead animals.

It takes some days to figure out the routine. I have to learn when to open gates, when to close them, when that sheep wants out and this one wants alfalfa cubes, what to feed the meat chickens, that the laying hens and their possessive roosters need to be rounded up well before sunset, that it's the breed not the hue of the feathers that determines egg colour. I learn that the cheerful sound of the sheep herd's twenty-two neck bells suddenly jingling simultaneously is cause for alarm. Coyotes and cougars and bears, he says, are no match for the livestock, nor for humans. "Normally. Normally I always have an intact male to keep them bastards away. But what are you gonna do. I got my eye out. Anatolian shepherd is what my Spitzy was. Parasite bored into his brain so I had no choice. Shot him dead. Goddamn dog attacked me in my own kitchen. Damn near killed me." He shuffles behind me as I work, pushing the wheelchair like it's a walker. Or he sulks and stays inside. Some days he doesn't get out of bed. I suggest water or tea and he croaks at me to bugger the hell off. On appointment days a volunteer driver picks him up and I do the chores, wander the property, swim in the lake, and wait for him to return.

I want to ask Hazel how (parasites aside) we can be sure of the brain's reliability. Because the idea that a brain is accurate in discerning the veracity of its own acumen begs the question. I'm stunned at the clarity with which I see this, and then immediately doubt myself: Am I seeing a circular argument or is it only that my own arguing is circular? I'm using my damaged brain to postulate, foolishly presuming a brain like mine can come up with something erudite. Hazel says I'm no longer dependable. And maybe she's right. When I'm struck hard, a grouping of letters that moments before clearly represented an object or concept becomes, in an instant, a series of nonsensical symbols, recognizable but not coherent. What I want to ask her is how anyone can know which version of their brain's machinations is correct? She'll have an answer. And the fact that she is absolutely clear in her vision of reality is grounding if nothing else. I was with her when Chance was born. Her hand squeezing mine as she panted through tight lips and tried to do as I instructed: Inhale, exhale. Relax. Trust your body. Chance was born two months after Mark left her for a younger, peppier, non-pregnant, but similar-looking woman. In the end they did a C-section. Failure to dilate beyond three centimetres.

"His safety is paramount," Hazel told me as I got on the bus. For his third birthday I bought a hammer and nails. What's wrong with a *toy* hammer and wood pegs, Hazel said as she pried the tools from Chance's hands. And then he and I played hide and seek in the shopping mall until a headache stole my vision and robbed me of judgement. I wasn't sure if we were playing a game or if I'd disappeared. "You could have lost him!" Hazel shouted. But sending a three-year-old around the block on his bike, the riding of which he'd mastered mere months earlier? Just because he wanted to go? That! she said. That was the final straw! The dog was with him, I told her. He wasn't alone. I was sure he could do it. And he *did* do it. I used to hold him on my lap when we took the bus, my arms tight around his torso, face pressed into his hair. A child, a pliable, off-sweet-smelling, slightly naughty boy between yourself and possible disaster can shore a person up. "You of all people should know better!" Hazel shouted. "He's three, for god's sake! *Three!*"

"You have children?" I ask Mick.

"Goddamn buggers'll suck you dry. Jed Jackson's Candice up and married that Glencoe bloke. Swindled Jackson out of everything that was worth something. Motor home. Bloody chainsaw. Didn't stop at nothing."

I interpret this non-answer as yes and then he says he's not that crazy and I realize he means no. He tells me to cook up eggs already. "Trying to starve me? Is that what you're doing?"

And then one evening I see August on the news. It takes a long minute before I register that the woman on the screen is August Ballard. August from my high school years. August who said she'd stop at nothing to get what she wanted. She stays frozen in the top right of the screen while the newscaster—as perfectly coiffed and carefully put together as August—explains that these are only allegations. At this point nothing has been substantiated. August is VP for an international tech company. She sits on boards, chairs committees, hobnobs with the 1%. All this is reported in a flat tone, the newscaster's eyes carefully neutral. Then the picture of August disappears and we're told about a whistle-blower's latest revelations, protesters somewhere, a war that's raging far away, the stock market's volatility. Eventually the newscaster turns to the weatherman, smiles and says, "You're sending rain across the west, I understand?"

"Tell you stories but you never get the whole thing," Mick says. "It's all about the money, that's all's what it is. You believe that crap and you're nothing but a goddamn fool. You shoulda thought to bring boots. Gonna be raining the next three days is what they're saying. Look at that. Not that they get it right ever. Not hereabouts anyhow."

So far I've been wearing his boots to work outside, my feet knocking around inside the rubber. It's better than runners, better than flip-flops. You can't walk the field for the livestock excrement. "Sheep gotta be moved up the road to Jed Jackson's if we get that kinda rain," he says. This on account of the pond in front of the house. When the water rises, he tells me, the whole clearing turns into a wetland. "Foot rot," he says. "Be the death of them." We watch the weather map flash rapidly moving lines and symbols to indicate rain or wind or sun depending where in the country you're looking. It moves quickly and I see stars falling and feel one side of my face tingle as the first hint of a headache pokes at my right lobe. In grade twelve August told me to give up Le Chateau and start collecting a designer line. Anne Klein, she suggested. "Something you can build on." Bulimia, she said, was weight control, nothing more. She introduced me to *Penthouse Forum*, which we read to each other, sipping lukewarm beers. She showed me how to backcomb, how to use hairspray to hold the newly created volume. Mick's mouth falls open and his snores drown out the noise of an ad about Ford trucks. Built to last. I'm getting used to the pattern of his days. I ease him upright, hand under his arm as he snorts awake, muttering, "What are you doing! Damn fidgeting. Resting my eyes, goddamn it. You got what? You got me?" I hold his elbow and walk him to his room, where the bed's unmade. "Leave it alone," he told me the first day. "What the hell's the point bothering with that?" The carpet is a gold-beige pile that's worn flat and threadbare, the dresser is strewn with beer cans and pop cans, several cloudy Mason jars, clothes, crumpled papers, and under all that his rifle, the barrel cantilevered off the dresser's edge. He puts his teeth on the bedside table, where they look more pathetic than macabre. I take off his cap, help him out of his clothes. And he gives me the same look he always does when his limp, shrunken privates are exposed, his eyes wicked and hopeless at the same time. I pull the Depends up his thighs. "Good dreams," I tell him.

"Goddamn right," he says. When I first arrived he put his hand on the back of my thigh and squeezed. "You got what I need," he said. I pull the blankets up over his shoulders. It's warm enough in the house but there's no meat on him. He's cold every night. I think about Chance in his T-Rex pjs. His pullups. When a toddler can jump with two feet he's ready to be potty trained. It seems a reasonable premise. But Hazel said letting him run around the yard in his birthday suit was inappropriate and wouldn't speed things along. And then the headache seizes me completely. I hold the wall to find my room and can't think how birthday and suit fit together. What built to last means. If I dreamed August Ballard.

I'm laid low. Night and day and night in bed, leaning over to puke into a bucket, which he brings me after I miss the toilet the first time. "What kind of goddamn caregiver are you!" he shouts. I hear banging. I hear plaintive bleating, the slam of a door, again and again. I hear moaning and then crying. The second morning I remember who is crying, what is bleating, and why I must get up. He tells me to get my lazy ass down to the lake. "Cure what ails you," he says. He's bent double in his chair and hisses at me to piss right off.

So I go. Despite the press of pending rain. Despite the wobble in my head.

I fill the hay feeder and scatter grain into the sheep pen. They're matted and filthy, coats covered in dried shit, blunted tails looking like tar-covered carpet remnants. The little heads that guide their bulk make them look exceptionally stupid. They bleat at me like they're beggars. Rain will do them good, I think. Clean things up. So far the weather's held off, the air loaded and still. If Chance were here we'd chase chickens and make them squawk and flap their useless wings while he laughed himself silly. That boy.

At the end of the steep path that's all but completely overgrown, there's a short stretch of sand strewn with logs and driftwood, weeds and sickly saplings, and then the water opens blue and clean. Swimming has become a late afternoon habit. I get my feet wet, stirring up muck and silt. And then I strip and wade in, chest seizing as the cold chokes until I acclimatize. I push off and dunk my head, hands and feet and then arms and legs losing all feeling. I come unstuck from myself. Numbed. I smell nothing, my eyes are closed, my ears are dulled to sound and when I open my mouth the water has no taste. This suspension of my sensory receptors heightens acutely—perversely—my awareness of his pain. He's not going to make it. I know that, but I've not allowed myself to think it. I lie on my back, open my eyes and see the sky. It's like the beautiful waking you to the ugly. He's fading, holding where he can. Pretending. Telling me next summer he'll be felling the fir that looms beside the house. "It's gonna come down one of these days. Kill me in my bed." Every day he scouts for pregnant bitches, calling buddies who put him on to breeders or farmers or puppy mills. "Takes time to find a good one," he tells me. "Time and research and patience. Half year to find my Spitzy. Yep. Half a goddamn year." The sheep are going to need shearing, he says, and then siring. Each lamb brings in 100 bucks. "You gotta look after your assets," he says. "Everything costs money."

I think about weighing pros and cons, measuring cost-effectiveness, cost versus benefit, effort versus reward. Death by tree would be quick. Twenty-two shots with his rifle and the sheep would be taken care of. One shot and Coombs is put out of his misery. I want to tell Hazel there's a reason grandparents raise children. That you can be too close. I want to tell her about Mick's horses. When the first one died the second one was nameless. Near wasn't relevant without Far. Point of view provides perspective, I want to say. Emotional distance leaves room for objectivity. Just because head injuries are dangerous, and just because I had a head injury, that doesn't mean I'm dangerous. When it rains there are clouds in the sky but that doesn't mean that when there are clouds in the sky it must be raining. I want to say that danger is relative. That risk analysis is in my bones. That negatives offer positives. Limitations offer insights she can't imagine from her vantage point, that's what I want to say.

I dreamed last night that the house floated away, trees and sheep and all. Chance sat on the bow of the boat—in my dream the house had become a boat—and threw apples for the sheep, who ran across the water like Jesus. I want to tell Hazel that he'll eat what she puts in front of him if he's hungry enough. I scull and kick my feet. When I looked at the clouds and asked Chance if he saw the big bird that I was imagining in the great puffs of white, he said that's not a bird, Grandma, that's a raptor. Hazel is thirty-six years old. She specializes in internal medicine. I'm a good swimmer. I flip over, open my eyes under the water and see nothing distinct and it feels right, and good. Because why should I be able to see under water?

"Out of your depth" is an expression Paul used to use. I should call him. After the accident he offered me his and Sally's basement suite. "I'd like to know you're not alone," he said, "should something happen." We do divorce well, Paul and I. We laugh about that. And we agree that maybe we were just too young when we had a baby. That it broke what could have been us. I don't mind Sally. But I told him no thank you, and took to frequenting Hazel's place. Before the bicycle debacle he agreed that maybe Hazel was a little overprotective. We acknowledged that this was understandable given she was a single parent and a doctor. "Neurological conditions are highly unpredictable, Mum. I know what I'm talking about." I want to tell her life is highly unpredictable and that I could teach Chance to swim and wouldn't that mitigate at least some risk? You can drown in two inches of water I want to tell her. But she knows that.

When I get back up to the house Mick is bellowing. In the middle of the kitchen, leaning on the back of his chair, sweats around his ankles, diarrhoea hardening the length of his pale, hairless legs. "Where the hell you been! You know why you're here? Your goddamn job?" Later he says, "Cougars walk that cliff. They're up there looking for a tasty something or other, for sure. For sure." Nodding his head. I always have my eye on the cliff as I paddle my arms. His house up there, set back. A younger Mick might have been sitting among the trees, out of view, watching the naked woman practise her swimming strokes, that's what I think.

Every day I feed the sheep, let them out, clean the pen, feed the chickens, let them out, clean the coop. I collect eggs. I feed the meat chickens, which are white and ugly and which cower as I clean around them. Some days I pick raspberries or beans or lettuce leaves, whatever Mick orders, some days I weed the garden. One morning he tells me I better damn well start building burn piles or it's not going to happen. It's a few seconds before I realize he means the debris in the clearing, which is a rutted close-grazed field knotted with masses of buttercups and thistles and burdock, and pocked with stumps and branches. I wheel him as close to the clearing as I can. Blanket over his knees, he watches as I build a pile of rubbish out of dead wood and shrub-sized weeds. "Not there! What are you doing? That's not a weed!" He tells me the cat's missing again, or the roof needs sweeping, or isn't it about time I did some washing? Every few days I pull on rubber gloves and offer a dead rodent to Coombs who acknowledges nothing. I reset the traps. Sometimes the cat brings in a mouse. Once the tail twitched when I dropped the rodent into the cage. Coombs made quick work of it. Then he looked at me and blinked. Bored and contemptuous. Or grateful.

Mick wakes up muttering, goes to sleep the same way. "Sail the hell outta Dodge," he says.

The rain comes a week late and it's the end of the swollen air. "What I tell ya?" Mick says as we watch sheets wash the length of the windows. "They always get it wrong."

Jed Jackson calls to say why don't I come along when he herds the sheep? Ride to his place with him? Bets I'm feeling pretty darn cooped up. In the house all day all night dealing with a sick old man. I do chores, I tell him. I get out. I go swimming. So I heard, he says and I detect French in his inflection.

August Ballard appears on the news again. She's finally caved to media pressure and is making a statement. "There have been times in my life when circumstances I've witnessed or been part of have brought out the worst in people, and there have been times when situations have brought out the best. I believe in being attuned to intentions." As she talks her words cross the bottom of the screen and I can't make sense of them. Apologize and wrongdoing and inadvertent and innocent. I wonder if August is a person I knew, or if the memory of her is something I've made up. Bodies are tools, August used to tell me. "There's no way we should be afraid to use what we have." Men, she told me, prefer blow jobs to conversation. I used to help her with math.

I call Paul's place. Sally answers and lowers her voice to tell me it's good I called because the babysitter was doing drugs. Well, not the babysitter, but the babysitter's boyfriend. And Sally thinks it was just pot but maybe it was something more, she's not sure. "So now Chance is in daycare," she says. "Paul didn't call to tell you because Hazel says stress can aggravate your condition." But Sally's telling me anyway, she says, because

I have a right to know. She can only imagine how this must be for me. "When are you coming home?" she asks. Mick shouts that it's goddamn cold in the house and shouldn't I be putting wood on the stove instead of yakking on the phone? And the runs are shooting again, he's pretty sure that's what he's feeling. I search Google for links between drug use and childcare but the results are inconclusive. I text Hazel that daycare kids are more prone to illness, then sponge Mick's backside with soap and warm water while he leans forward, forearms pressed into the sink's edge. Hazel sends a photo of Chance between her and Paul, three mouths of white teeth gleaming well-being at me. Everything's good, she texts.

Jed Jackson tells me I'm crazy if I think we're gonna walk—I wanna walk behind sheep for six kilometres? In the rain? So I get in his truck, slide my hands under my thighs and pinch tight the skin. I'll close my eyes, I tell myself. I'll count backward from 100 and then do it again. There's rarely traffic on this road. We're in the middle of nowhere. Three hours from the nearest city. Two kilometres from the hamlet, which is made up of twelve houses, a defunct motel, an equally defunct gas station, a boarded-up ranger's station, and a dark, double-wide trailer which operates as corner store, liquor store and post office, and has a coin-operated washer and two dryers on the makeshift porch out back. It's closed if the weather is inclement. I've walked to the store eight times to pick up this or that and the woman has yet to acknowledge me. There's dust on the cans and on the Minute Rice and cereal boxes that line the shelves in random fashion. Once she had bananas. No car is going to crash into us.

The sheep cluster and jingle ahead of the truck. My eyes are open. Rain on the windshield softens the view and the sheep look dirtier than they did before the weather changed.

"How you making out?" Jed Jackson asks. He's lean, younger than me by five years or so. I tell him okay, thinking he's referring to his driving and the relative comfort of the truck. He knows I don't like vehicles, but he doesn't know why. Doesn't know it's a full-blown phobia. But then he goes on and I realize he's asking about my living arrangement. "Not going crazy by yourself with old man Mick?" His hand rests on the seat between us and it's a hard-working hand, the lines in the skin creased black, the thumbnail purple-blue and ridged, coming loose from its bed. "That" he pronounces "dat." French Canadian is an accent I remember from when I was eight years old and my parents left me and my brother with a family of strangers in rural Quebec for a week while they drove to the Maritimes.

"*Es-tu Québécois?*"

He nods. "*Oui.* On my mother's side."

I make him laugh with the story about my mother and the family she didn't know. "They were decent people, she said. They had nine children. That had to mean something. And the week was bound to be good for our French."

"Strangers?" he says. "You would be forced to speak? This is what she was thinking?"

"*Oui,*" I say. "But for some reason, my brother and I didn't learn *beaucoup* French. We learned to eat quickly. We learned to fold laundry and do dishes." I like seeing him laugh.

"Ah, well." He winks and then holds eye contact. "Maybe it's not about the language for the French, eh?"

In *Penthouse Forum* there was a story about a truck and a stick shift. August told me women use all kinds of things. "*Peut être,*" I say. I ease my hands out from under my thighs and set my feet wider on the floor. He puts his hand on my leg and I go warm under the solidness of contact. My body is rushing itself toward this man. Olfactory senses leading. When I got in the truck it was diesel and dirt but now, out of nowhere, it's a soap smell from my past. Not long after he met Sally, Paul came over and found me in the laundry room, my arms elbow-deep in magnolia-scented suds, massaging clean my merino sweater. That was our last go at passion. The sheep trot ahead, their backs broad as a picnic blanket. Not one runs rogue. A solid mass of dull, filthy-white wool broken by the occasional black anomaly. If the truck stopped, if Jed Jackson turned the motor off, we'd hear their bells.

"I heard you was weird," he says. "This can be a very good thing, weird." He looks at me a second too long so that the truck shudders onto the soft shoulder and my hands fly to the dash. Eyes shut tight. The unstable jolt, the slide, Jed's sudden tension, my history, all of it rushes in. From every side. I can't breathe and my brain shrinks and beside me Jed Jackson whoops about taking a gamble, living dangerously, logging trucks and playing chicken and how them bastards will push you right off the road if they smell fear. "Just like this!" he shouts. "You feel this? How close we come to rollover?"

He coaxes the listing truck to firmer ground. Glint in his eye, hand back on my leg, hard and purposeful.

I press tight the sides of my head. To hold it together. My brain. And when my breath is back where it belongs, my voice comes out in a whisper. "Do you realize?" But what am I trying to say? I'm not sure if he has no control or if I have no control. Or if nobody does. Or if we do. "I have a daughter," I say. "I have a grandson." Chance in daycare, being looked after by strangers.

"Whoa," Jed Jackson says. "What the hell's got in you?"

I can feel his single-mindedness, his frustration, his easy ability to navigate or ignore, whichever suits.

"I want to go back," I say. "I need to."

"Yeah, well, we got the sheep," Jed Jackson says. And then he keeps his eyes on me and slams his fist on the truck's horn. Holds it down so that the sheep are jarred out of conformity, startled and confused.

My hands shoot to the dash again. Small breaths, small breaths.

Jed Jackson whistles through his teeth, eyebrows raised, mouth twitching with the beginnings of laughter. He releases the horn and the sheep resume their tempered gait. I let go of the dash. Push my hands tight under my legs and focus on the slap of the wipers. A squeak on one side and a downbeat on the other. What I remember about the family in Quebec is they sat at the dinner table together and prayed before and after the meal, holding hands. I didn't speak to my mother for two years. The reason I've forgotten, but the rift was irreparable. I need to go home.

I should try to explain, but instead I open the door and Jed Jackson is forced to stop, shouting, "What the fuck are you doing?"

I get out. And despite what's become a downpour, despite my useless footwear, I run. Slow, steady, desperate steps. Please, Mick, I pray. Because he could be on the floor, crumpled, he could be out cold, trusting in his unconscious brain that I'll be back. Please, Chance. Please, Mick. The whole way down that gravel road I run and pray. Because Mick's collapsed, I'm sure of it. Or he might collapse. And I need to talk to Hazel. To explain that people might be unreasonable because they're scared. That maybe fear trumps logic. I need to tell her that intention means something even if it becomes irrelevant. That I don't know. That I hope. Because what more can I do? In the dimming light the tree trunks are darker and more ominous. Obfuscated. This is a word I know. Running entices a cougar to leap. I know this too. But I run, feet slapping wet and loud. The beat of contrition.

Mick is asleep. In front of the TV, where he always is this time of day. The cat bolts from his lap, past my legs and gone. I stand in the doorway to catch my breath and then I cross the room and lift Mick's arm to straighten his shoulders. His head has a habit of lolling left, useless as a doll's. "Goddamn Jed Jackson!" he shouts, starting awake. "Bloody bastard that guy! I tell you he's a bastard? I tell you that?" I help him to the bathroom and watch the erratic pivot onto the toilet. The sound of him voiding is so weak, so pathetic. He's goddamn tired, he says, don't I know he needs a lie-down? And so I walk him to the bedroom, his hand holding my arm, his weight against me. He is light and his breathing is heavy. I help him sit, ease his legs onto the bed.

"What the hell's wrong with you? Why you so cold?" He swats at my hands. "You're goddamn dripping," he says. "Get away! Leave me alone!"

I tell him it's the rain. I walked back, I say. I can't control the break in my voice. Hazel lives in a quiet neighbourhood. There's a speed limit of thirty. But if the bike had wobbled? If he fell? If a driver looked left when he should have looked right? A loose pebble on the road and just like that everything changes. I weighed the odds and then I got in the back seat of that tuk-tuk. I wipe my eyes and face with my sleeve. "Sorry," I say. "I'm sorry."

He looks at me, scrutinizing. And then he shakes his head and looks at his lap. "Where's the cat at?" he says. "You go letting her out?" Straining to get his feet back on the floor, fighting my attempts to assist. "Where the hell's the cat?"

She comes when I call, darting in as fast as she went out. I've never seen her eat. Never seen signs of her scat. She flits through walls is what it feels like. On his lap or gone completely. She touches her nose to his shoulder, his cheek, then moves to the foot of the bed. "Damned critters," he says. My hands guide him onto his back. I've taken off his ball cap. His teeth are on the bedside table. My throat is thick. I want to tell him that an exit strategy offers hope. Even if it doesn't float. I want to say that I looked into the owl's eyes.

"They know a helluva lot more'n you think," he says. "Helluva lot. You betcha."

I'm not sure if his eyes are watering or tearing, if he's looking at me or at nothing, but what I feel is the primeval tug of compassion. It's unmistakable. I feel it with my whole body. The way it opens me.

ABOUT THE AUTHOR

Meg Todd is a B.C. writer whose stories have been recognized in Canada and the United States. Her work was shortlisted for the CBC literary prize (2017, 2019), *New Letters* Robert Day Award (2019) and *CRAFT*'s short fiction prize (2020). She grew up on the Alberta prairies and holds an MFA in Creative Writing from the University of British Columbia. She lives on Vancouver Island.

Eco-Audit
*Printing this book using Rolland Enviro 100 Book
instead of virgin fibres paper saved the following resources:*

Trees	Water	Air Emissions
3	1,000 L	202 kg